Newcastle
City Council

Newcastle Libraries and Information Service

 0845 002 0336

Due for return	Due for return	Due for return

Please return this item to any of Newcastle's Libraries by the last
date shown above. ff not requested by another customer the loan
can be renewed, you can do this by phone, post or in person.
Charges may be made for late returns.

KINGFISHER
An imprint of Kingfisher Publications Plc
New Penderel House, 283-288 High Holborn
London WC1V 7HZ
www.kingfisherpub.com

First published by Kingfisher 2006
2 4 6 8 10 9 7 5 3 1

Text copyright © Working Partners Ltd 2006
Created by Working Partners Limited, London W6 0QT
Cover illustration copyright © Angelo Rinaldi 2006

The moral right of the author has been asserted.

A CIP catalogue record for this book
is available from the British Library.

ISBN-13: 978 0 7534 1091 2
ISBN-10: 0 7534 1091 5

Printed in India
1TR/0506/THOM/MA/90GSM(W)/C

★ SADDLE THE WIND ★

ON THE EDGE OF
REVOLUTION

DEBORAH KENT

KINGFISHER

✶ Chapter One ✶

Eliza Carter paced down the long flour mill yard and stopped at Clipper's side. The big black gelding shifted restlessly in the traces of his harness. He greeted her with a snort and the impatient stamp of his forefeet.

"I know how you feel," Eliza said, patting his massive flank. "I want to get going too."

All day Eliza and her brothers had worked beneath the fierce August sun, helping Henry Smithfield's crew load up the three specially built Conestoga wagon beds with sacks of freshly ground flour. The four horses were harnessed and eager to begin the haul back to the Carter warehouse. Henry Smithfield had already given her oldest brother, Benjamin, the receipt – properly signed. Yet the two of them still stood alongside the wagons, lost in conversation.

Eliza slipped a hand under the wagon's grey canvas hood and felt the heavy roundness of one of the sacks. They had loaded twelve tons altogether, according to Henry Smithfield's careful calculations. Eliza tried to imagine how much bread twelve tons of flour could make – she thought of mountains of hot golden loaves, crusty and plump, sliding out of ovens. Since early spring farmers all over the Philadelphia valley had ploughed and sowed, hoed weeds and driven away crows, and finally cut down the wheat sheaves and winnowed the grain to take to the mill. Then Smithfield turned the grain into flour, ready for distribution. All those months of toil culminated here, with the Carter wagons loaded and waiting to move forward. Only a Conestoga wagon could carry such an enormous load, and only a carefully trained team of Conestoga horses could pull the wagon to its destination.

Jeremy, Eliza's twin brother, sauntered up with his hands in his pockets. Eliza saw tension in his jaw and around his eyes. He didn't have to say that he was annoyed with Ben for talking for so long – she could read it in his face.

Eliza gestured toward Benjamin and Smithfield. "Business? Still?"

Jeremy nodded, as she knew he would. "Prices and profits," he grumbled, kicking a stone. "What about principles?"

Eliza watched Jeremy look up at the sky. They probably had less than three hours until dark. "You're right — we need to be on the road," she said, though Jeremy hadn't spoken his thoughts aloud. "I'll tell Ben that we had better hurry."

Jeremy shrugged. "He might listen to you," he said. "He doesn't listen to me these days, that's for sure."

Eliza winced, but she said nothing. She wanted to believe that her brothers were as close as they had always been, but since she had come back from boarding school in May, it was hard to ignore the growing strain between them. With a parting pat for Clipper, she set off across the yard.

"…rumours flying around the country like pigeons," Smithfield was saying. "Somebody fires a shot in Boston, and by the time we hear the story down here, it was a full-blown battle with one hundred men dead."

Ben was listening intently. He was a half head taller

than Jeremy, broad and muscular where Jeremy was wiry and slim. Ben's hair was dark – almost black – while the twins, in true twin fashion, were both reddish blondes. But all three were unmistakably Carters. They shared their papa's high cheekbones and his strong, confident jaw. They had his smile, too, and his good-natured laugh. Not that any of them had been laughing much lately, though, Eliza knew. Somehow life lately was becoming too solemn for anyone's good.

Ben nodded to Smithfield. "They talk about those killings they call the Boston Massacre as if it happened yesterday," he said. "That was four years ago, back in 1770!"

"The way I see it," Smithfield told him, "the king sending more soldiers means we'll have more business. The army has to eat. We all stand to gain."

"Ben," Eliza said gently. "Will you be much longer?"

Ben glanced up, startled, and seemed to remember the time. "We're leaving right now," he assured her. With a hasty goodbye to the miller, he followed Eliza back to the wagons.

Each one of the three big blue wagons was more than twenty feet in length, and drawn by a team of four Conestoga horses. With all three wagons loaded to capacity, the process of getting underway required patience and care. Eliza sprang up onto Clipper's back and looked over her shoulder to be certain that the rest of the team was on the alert. Clipper was the lead horse, positioned in the front left of the formation – the driver controlled the horses from the left-side, and kept to the right hand side of the road, in order to keep an eye on the road ahead and any oncoming wagons. The other three horses – all powerful Conestogas like Clipper himself – waited expectantly.

"Same formation as when we drove over?" Ben asked.

"Right," Jeremy answered. "Maura brings up the rear. She's happy when no one's behind her."

"So I'll be in the middle with Hansel," Ben agreed, "and Clipper in the lead, naturally."

"Naturally!" Eliza said, grinning. Sometimes it was still hard to believe that Clipper had proved to be the finest lead horse that the Carter Grain Company owned.

Two years ago her papa had been ready to sell him off cheaply to the first buyer who came along. As a saddle horse Clipper had been eager and responsive, but in harness, he had balked. As a wheelhorse or swing horse he needed constant urging and correcting, and his bad example caused the other horses to be on their worst behaviour.

Eliza remembered the morning her father unhitched Clipper in disgust and turned him out into the field. "He's impossible!" he declared. "Not worth the hay it takes to feed him."

"Don't sell him yet!" Eliza had pleaded. "Let me work with him and see what happens. He's such a good saddle horse; I know he can learn."

"He's a Conestoga, not a lady's palfrey," Papa had reminded her. "Some horses just don't have proper sense. I'm afraid Clipper is one of them." But Eliza wouldn't give up, and finally Papa had agreed to let her train Clipper for a week before he offered him for sale. "I almost hate to pass him on to someone else," he'd admitted. "A horse like that can give the Carter stables a bad name."

Now Clipper stood in the lead position, his muscles taut, his head held high and alert as he waited for Eliza's command. "Haw!" she cried, nudging his right flank with her heel. Obediently he swung left onto the road. Behind him the rest of the team leaned into harness, their bells ringing merrily. With a creak of axles and a grinding of wheels on gravel, the wagon began to move. Benjamin came next with Hansel's team, and Jeremy completed the procession, guiding the team that was led by the big dun mare, Maura. The mighty hooves of twelve huge Conestogas pounded the hard-packed earth of the roadway, while the wagons groaned under the weight of their massive loads.

Eliza recalled her first morning training Clipper on her own. She had hitched him to one of the wagons with a team led by a big bay gelding named Zeus. Clipper had been as stubborn and uncooperative as usual, but Eliza had refused to be discouraged. She had tried to imagine what Clipper experienced when he was in the traces. Perhaps he didn't like the pressure of the harness across his chest or the rumble of the wagon wheels behind him. Maybe he felt nervous with the other horses crowded in so close around him. After all, as a saddle horse he was on his own, with no other horses ahead or beside him. Perhaps he needed the independence.

That was when the idea had sprang into Eliza's mind. Maybe Clipper was meant to be a lead horse! It amazed her that no one had tried this before. Sure enough, when she had harnessed him in the lead position, switching him with Zeus, he had held his head up high and set off at a brisk trot. Zeus had been reluctant to follow him at first, as though he could not understand why his prized position had been given to such a troublesome horse. However, within a mile or two the bay had accepted Clipper's leadership. Eliza sensed that she was on the right track.

Even so, Clipper had been slow to follow directions. As her father had taught her, Eliza rode the left wheelhorse, April, and held a long rein with which to control Clipper ahead of her. Sometimes, though, when he was in high spirits and felt the wagon gliding smoothly behind him, Clipper didn't seem to notice Eliza pulling his rein at all. It had been as though he felt that he was bearing the full responsibility for the whole team, as well as the wagon and all its contents. He had the same powerful confidence as he had when he was a saddle horse. But Eliza had realised that if she was on his back, he would instantly respond to her commands.

Again an idea had formed in Eliza's mind. What would happen if she rode Clipper instead of April? With some difficulty she had pulled the team to a halt there and then. When all four horses stood still in the road, stamping and blowing, she switched April's saddle to Clipper's broad back. Clipper watched her curiously as she cinched the girth, and he gave a questioning little whinny.

"Just pay attention when I tell you which way to go," she had said firmly. "Listen to me, and you'll do fine."

Using a tree stump as a mounting block – Clipper stood seventeen hands high – Eliza sprang into the saddle and gathered up the reins. With a cluck of her tongue, she had nudged him forward with her heels. Clipper had responded without hesitation, as he always did when she rode him.

"Gee!" she had called, pressing her heel into his left flank. Clipper made the right turn with plenty of room for the rest of the team and the cumbersome wagon to follow him. It was as if he knew by instinct how to time the turn, giving the wagon exactly the space that it needed.

Eliza loved to remember the astonished look on her father's face when she had ridden Clipper back to the wagon yard at the head of the team, the gaits of the four horses matched perfectly, as though they were one.

"To think I called him worthless!" he kept exclaiming. "With all my years in the business, it took a girl of twelve to set me straight!"

Now, two years later, Papa loved to tell people Clipper had no equal as a lead horse and was so intelligent that he knew his own mind.

Brought out of her memories by a fork in the road, Eliza reined Clipper to a halt as they approached the turnoff to Grimsby Place. Her brothers stopped their teams behind her, and she pointed off to the right.

"Maybe we should ford the stream down there," she suggested. "Taking a shortcut would save a lot of time."

"We'd be taking a chance," Ben said, frowning. "We'll have a disaster on our hands if one of the wagons overturns in the water."

At once Jeremy joined in on Eliza's side. "It will be almost dark by the time we go all the way to the bridge," he insisted. "We crossed at the ford in June, remember?"

"The wagons weren't so heavy then," Ben pointed out. "This is different."

"I've ridden Clipper across the ford lots of times," Eliza said. "He's used to it, and the other horses follow him."

Ben studied the sky, pondering. Eliza and Jeremy exchanged a knowing look, and Eliza was sure that they were thinking the same thing – if Ben hadn't spent so long talking, they would have left the mill in plenty of time.

"All right," Ben said at last. "Let's try the ford."

The three wagons turned to the right, breaking away from the main road to proceed along a narrow, rutted track through the woods. The path was broken up by rocks and stumps, but the sturdy, wide-wheeled wagons rolled along unperturbed. They were designed for the rugged roads in colonial Pennsylvania, and Eliza knew that they could handle much worse than this.

As they topped a rise, Eliza heard the splash of tumbling water ahead. Rain had been scarce for the past two weeks, and the stream was not deep. The water wouldn't come up to Clipper's knees, but the swift current and the slippery stony bottom meant that they would have to be careful.

"Even the bank on this side is steep, Eliza," Ben called out to her. "We should do this single file."

Eliza nodded and brought Clipper to a complete stop to let him survey the terrain before them. Ben was right; they had never crossed here with such heavily-loaded wagons before. Still she was certain that Clipper could manage, and she knew that the other horses would follow wherever he led.

Eliza dismounted and fastened the lock chain to the rear wheels to keep the wagon from gathering too much momentum as it descended the bank. Ben and Jeremy did the same – all of them schooled by years of experience. When she was sure that everything was ready, she mounted again and urged Clipper forward. Slowly, deliberately, he stepped onto the slope. All the strength of his great body focussed on moving the wagon steadily ahead. Every step seemed to be the right one, and the rest of the team followed fearlessly.

They were in the water now, Clipper's hooves ringing on the stones at the bottom of the stream. The water rippled and foamed around his mighty legs as he strode toward the far bank. It was slow but steady progress.

By the time Clipper climbed ashore, the front wheels of the wagon were halfway across. Curved at the front and rear, the wagon looked like a boat floating above the surface of the water.

When the wagon safely rolled onto dry land again, Eliza reined in Clipper to wait for her brothers. In a few minutes Ben and his wagon came to join her.

"Atta girl, Maura," Jeremy was saying behind them. "Easy there – it's only water!"

Maura eased her way down the bank and took her first careful steps into the water. She was a good follower, solid and uncomplaining. Eliza knew that she preferred to keep her feet dry, but when Jeremy ordered her into a stream, she obeyed him without reproach.

Suddenly, Eliza heard a sickening crunch, and Maura's wagon tilted dangerously to the right side. Maura came to an abrupt standstill, her ears twitching nervously as Jeremy leaped down to inspect the damage.

"It's the front right wheel!" he groaned. "Split on a rock somehow."

Eliza and Ben hurried to see for themselves. The great wooden wheel, which had borne its share of the wagon's huge weight, had almost splintered in two.

Eliza surveyed the wagon in dismay. *So much for saving time*, she thought gloomily. *So much for taking the shortcut!* If only she'd kept quiet, they'd have gone around to the bridge and been home for supper.

"No real harm done," Jeremy said, sensing her anxiety. "At least none of the sacks slid off."

"They still might, unless we get this wheel changed," Ben said.

He opened the chest of tools that hung from Jeremy's wagon and pulled out a jack. Crouching in the water as they worked, Ben and Jeremy managed to lift the wagon into an upright position again within a few minutes. Now they could all see the broken wheel more clearly. Eliza felt certain that Papa would be able to mend it back home in his workshop, but there was no way that they could get the wagon home with one wheel so badly cracked.

"I should have brought a spare," Jeremy said, running a hand through his hair.

"Don't worry, I have one," Ben said. "Let's see what we can do."

The broken wheel defied their best efforts at first, stubbornly clinging to the axle and refusing to release its hold. Eliza could see that the job would require time and patience – and both were in short supply.

"And now we get to the real job," Jeremy said when Ben finally pulled the wheel free. "It's not easy to do this, even on dry land."

They had had a long, exhausting day, and now they were wet and hungry as well. When the sun went down, they would be cold too, on top of everything else. Eliza tried not to think about that. She held the wheel as steadily as she could, while the boys struggled to manoeuvre it into place.

"The jack is starting to buckle!" Ben exclaimed. "We'll have to find a log to help hold the wagon up."

It was true. The wagon was starting to tilt again. If the jack failed to hold, the whole wagon could overturn, dumping its precious load of flour into the stream.

Suddenly Eliza heard the sound of hooves on the path above them. Two men approached on horseback. "Hello!" the riders called. "Need any help?"

"Mr Werner!" Eliza cried in delight. "We have a broken wheel!"

Rudolf Werner dismounted and tethered his horse to a branch. He was a tall, brawny farmer with greying hair and hints of German in his speech. Eliza had known the Werners all her life. She and Harriet Werner had been friends since they were seven, and for two years they had both attended Miss Halsey's Academy – a boarding school for girls in Philadelphia.

The other rider she recognised as John Robinson. He was younger and leaner than Mr Werner and had a deep, steady gaze that seemed to peer beneath the surface of things. The Robinson farm lay deep in the woods, and John Robinson and his family didn't come to town often. They were the sort of people who generally kept to themselves.

From the moment the farmers arrived, the repair of the wagon turned from an ordeal into a party.

"Thought you would whip up a few cakes out here?" Mr Werner teased Eliza. "Flour, water – what more do you need?"

The men crowded in to assess the situation, and Eliza stepped out of their way. Papa and her brothers respected her ability to drive a team and handle a wagon, but to the rest of the world she was still just a girl who belonged in the kitchen with her mother. Her brothers didn't need her help with the wheel now that two grown men had arrived. For a few minutes she watched the work from a little distance away. When it was clear that everything was going smoothly, she walked along the line of wagons to check on the horses.

Eliza was working a stone out of Clipper's right rear hoof when again she heard the thud of approaching riders. Looking up, she saw three red-coated British soldiers galloping toward her. They reined in their horses at the edge of the stream. "Lost a wheel, have you?" asked the man in the lead.

"Just a little mishap," Ben said, smiling. "Smashed it

on a rock."

The soldier nodded his sympathy. "Can we be of assistance?"

"I don't think so," John Robinson said shortly and bent down to his work again.

"Well, maybe you could just—" Ben began.

"We're fine as we are," Jeremy interrupted. "*We locals can take care of ourselves.*"

Eliza stared at him, shocked. It wasn't like Jeremy to be rude. No matter what he thought of the new soldiers from London, he ought to be gracious to these men who offered their help.

"Suit yourselves, then," the soldier said. Without another word the three red-coated riders splashed across the stream and disappeared into the woods on the other side.

"What was that about?" Ben demanded when the soldiers were out of earshot.

"Just what I said," Jeremy told him. "We don't need any help from the king's men."

"He's right," John Robinson added. "The less we have to do with them, the better."

"If they really wanted to help us," Mr Werner said, "they'd go back to where they came from."

"We're all subjects of King George," Ben reminded them. "If it weren't for the king's protection, we'd still be fighting the Indians."

"Protection!" Jeremy repeated in disgust. "Pretty soon they'll be 'protecting' Philadelphia the way they 'protect' Boston."

Eliza felt her body growing tense, the way it always did when her brothers argued. "Stop it!" she said sternly. "We have twelve tons of grain to take home!"

"Don't worry your sister with politics," Mr Werner said, adjusting the axle. "There – that wheel should be fine now. She'll run smooth like honey from a spoon."

Even Ben chuckled at the turn of phrase, and Eliza felt the tension ease. The new wheel was on, and when Jeremy prompted Maura, the wagon rolled forward as though nothing had ever gone amiss.

As they shouted their thanks and continued homeward, Eliza could almost believe that life was back to normal once more. But she could not forget the bite of anger in Jeremy's voice when he declared, *We locals can take care of ourselves.*

⋆ Chapter Two ⋆

"Can I help?" Mary asked, as Eliza braided a piece of blue yarn into Clipper's forelock. A pompom swung from each end like a puffy cloud.

Eliza's finger traced the white blaze on Clipper's forehead. She eyed her younger sister doubtfully. Mary was seven — what their mother called "a curious age". Sometimes she was more interested in mischief than being of real use. Still, Eliza couldn't resist her pleading brown eyes.

"All right," she said, handing her the horse brush. "Gently now."

Clipper stood patiently as Mary glided the brush over his left flank. *They'll do all right together*, Eliza decided.

As Eliza moved to the next stall to check on April, Mary suddenly asked, "Can you teach a horse to sit up or roll over like a dog?"

"Why would anyone want to?" Eliza asked, laughing. "A horse has serious work to do."

After their hard day yesterday the horses in the three Carter teams were getting a well-earned rest. The day was their own. They stood in their stalls, munching or dozing, while Eliza made her rounds, tending to each one in a row. She cleaned their hooves, checked for sores from harness rub, combed the burrs and straw from their manes, and brushed their coats until they glistened.

"Horses are smarter than dogs, don't you think?" Mary persisted. "They should be able to learn tricks."

Eliza pondered. "Horses have savvy," she said. "They understand roads and trails and hauling wagons. Those are the things that matter to them." And loyalty, she wanted to add. They know who cares about them, who they can trust.

Before she could shape her thoughts into words, Eliza heard the clatter of hooves in the drive. "Anyone here?" a man's voice boomed. "Where's the master of the house?"

Eliza hurried out into the sunlight. Three men had ridden into the wagon yard. They wore ruffled shirts and black hats with jaunty, upturned brims. These were not ordinary farmers but gentlemen! With a gasp of surprise, she recognised the tall, blond figure who dismounted and strode toward her.

"Governor Penn!" she exclaimed, dropping a nervous curtsy. "Can I help you?"

For years the Carters had done business with the estates of the Penn family – the proprietors of Pennsylvania. The Penns established Pennsylvania almost 100 years ago and governed the colony on and off ever since, along with a council of locals. John Penn, the current lieutenant governor of the Pennsylvania Colony, had only recently arrived from London, and since then Eliza had often driven with her father or one of her brothers to the governor's mansion in Philadelphia, delivering flour and vegetables from the countryside. But she couldn't remember a time when any of the governors had ever come out to Judsonville to pay them a visit. What was happening today that brought him to their door?

The governor removed his hat and wiped his forehead with a lace-trimmed handkerchief. Like every proper gentleman, he wore a small, powdered wig underneath. *No wonder he's hot*, Eliza thought.

Penn wasted no time with pleasantries. "Is your father at home?" he asked. "I need to speak with him."

"Mary!" Eliza called. "Find Papa and tell him to come right away!"

Mary popped out of the barn. With fascination, she stared at the governor and his men. "Go find Papa!" Eliza repeated. "Now!"

In an instant Mary was off, dashing to the west field. *She'll find Papa,* Eliza assured herself, *and he will get to the barn as quickly as he can.* In the meantime their esteemed visitor was her responsibility.

"Would you like to go inside?" she asked, gesturing toward the house. "Are you hungry after your ride?"

"I'd like to take a look at your horses," the governor stated, waving her offer aside. "Are the teams in the barn today?"

"Yes, they're all here," Eliza said. The governor followed her into the barn, trailed by his watchful companions. He walked up and down the row of stalls, pausing to admire each one of the big Conestogas.

"I like what I see," he remarked, and his normally stern features warmed with a smile. "Which is your strongest lead horse?"

"Clipper is," Eliza said proudly, pointing him out. "Everyone knows it. Sometimes when a farmer has an especially big harvest, he asks for Clipper's team in particular."

"Were all these horses bred right here, in your family's stables?" the governor asked.

If Governor Penn wanted to hear about horses, Eliza would have no trouble finding things to say. "Yes, sir. They were all bred right here," she told him. "My mother's family, the Wintons, had some big Flemish horses, the kind the first Quakers – your family – brought over here in the early days. They bred them with some stock from the Virginia plantations – good, wiry horses that did well in the American climate – and they developed the Conestogas. They're wonderful horses!" she added. "They learn fast, and when they know you and trust you, they'll do anything you ask. Papa says they have a lot of wisdom."

The governor shifted restlessly, and Eliza saw that his gaze was wandering. "How much can one of your teams haul?" he asked abruptly.

"Up to six tons," she said, "if the wagon's loaded the right way."

Governor Penn nodded with satisfaction. "That should do very nicely," he said, turning to his men. "Let's see what we can arrange."

"He's coming! I found him! He's almost here!" cried Mary, dashing into the barn. Her ribbons had come undone, and her hair fluttered loose around her face.

Papa was only a few steps behind her, his face flushed from running. "This is a great honour," he said to the governor, holding out his hand. "What brings you out this way?"

"I'm on my way to visit the garrison at Germantown," the governor explained. "There's a fresh battalion coming out here to protect the city, and we need to get ready for them."

"More troops from England?" Papa asked. "Does the Crown really need to send more soldiers to our little colony?"

"The Crown doesn't want another Boston on its hands," Governor Penn said grimly. "If trouble is brewing, we'll have to take measures."

"Of course," Papa said, nodding. "But we haven't come to that yet, have we? Pennsylvania's a long way from Massachusetts."

"We've had the port of Boston blockaded since

March," the governor reminded him. "Those rebels up there should be starved out by now. We know they're getting help. There are rebels in Pennsylvania and Virginia and all over the colonies sympathetic to their so-called cause."

Papa gave a vague nod. "Is there anything we can do for you today?" he asked, changing the subject. "A shipment we can take care of?"

Governor Penn went straight to his purpose. "I'm here to buy a team for the King's Regulars," he announced. "They'll be hauling a lot of supplies, and they need to have teams they can rely on."

Eliza reeled back in shock. The family shipping business, the Carter Distribution Company, depended on its teams. The horses were her family's livelihood. To sell one of the teams was unthinkable! She studied her father's face, trying to gauge his reaction, but his expression wasn't clear. Papa would never willingly part with one of his teams, she knew — but neither would he dare to offend the lieutenant governor.

"I'm afraid we can't afford to sell," Papa said slowly. "Our business keeps all three teams busy. We don't have any to horses spare."

"I'll give you a price that will make it worth your

while," Governor Penn said with a touch of annoyance. "I need your four best horses and a good strong Conestoga wagon."

"If you have a particular job in mind, we'll contract to do the work for you," Papa said reasonably. "Let me know what you need."

"I promised to have a team ready for the garrison's commanding officer," the governor said. "I understand this big fellow over here is your best team leader."

In consternation Eliza watched the governor walk directly to Clipper's stall. She had boasted to him that Clipper was the best leader they had. Now he meant to take Clipper away!

Eliza fastened her eyes upon Papa's face and willed him to understand her. He couldn't sell Clipper! He simply couldn't! She and Clipper belonged together. They couldn't be separated, not even to please the lieutenant governor and the king's battalion.

"Beautiful!" the governor murmured. "Look at those legs – pure power!"

"He's a beauty all right," Papa agreed. "One of our finest." He paused, and Eliza held her breath. "But he's tough to handle," her father went on. "You can ask my daughter – he's got a real stubborn streak."

"He sure has!" Eliza chimed in enthusiastically. "If he doesn't like the way you guide him, he'll bring the whole team to a dead stop."

The governor frowned. "No, we can't have that," he said, and Eliza felt a surge of relief. "We need a team we can count on."

"Maybe we could work out an arrangement with the garrison," Papa suggested. "We could contract to deliver their supplies, using our own teams."

Governor Penn shook his head. "The garrison wants its own team," he explained. "Besides, I know how busy you are at this time of year. The other day I was talking to my brother-in-law, Simon Billings – he mentioned that he uses the Carter wagons to haul his grain to the mill." The governor looked pointedly at Papa as he spoke. "Of course, he can consider other possibilities, but as it stands, he prefers to go with your company – unless something unforeseen changes."

Eliza winced at the threat behind the governor's words: something unforeseen might happen if the Carters refused to sell one of their teams. Simon Billings would take his business to someone else, and there were plenty of other farmers who might do the same if the governor wanted them to. As the proprietor of Pennsylvania, Governor Penn wielded influence in the country around Philadelphia, and he didn't hesitate to use it.

"The big black fellow is stubborn, you say," the governor went on. "Show me a leader you can recommend."

"Take a look at Maura over here," Papa said. "She's as steady as they come, and she'll work for anyone."

They entered Maura's stall, and Papa launched into a list of her virtues. She was strong and sure-footed. Nothing ever frightened her. She was an experienced leader, and the other horses respected her. The garrison couldn't go wrong with Maura and her team.

The governor smiled and nodded. "All right," he said at last. "Let's go outside and discuss the terms."

Flanked by his pair of assistants, the governor led the way out of the barn. Eliza stood by the horse trough, only half listening. She was deeply grateful to Papa for sparing Clipper – but she couldn't imagine the Carter stables without big, patient Maura. And how would they manage with only two teams to carry out the work of three? Didn't Governor Penn understand what a blow this loss would be to their family? Did he even care?

Eliza heard footfalls on the grass and looked up to see Jeremy and Ben coming toward her. Ben joined their father and the governor, while Jeremy came to stand beside Eliza.

"What are they doing here?" he whispered.

"They came…" Eliza struggled to say the terrible words, ". . . to buy one of the teams. For the garrison."

"They can't!" Jeremy cried. "Papa won't let them!"

Eliza took Jeremy's arm and led him far out of earshot. "Papa has to sell," she said miserably. "Otherwise Penn will get Simon Billings to take his business away from us – probably other farmers, too. He can ruin us if he wants to."

"That's just what he wants us to think," Jeremy said with a bitter laugh. "They want us to be afraid – that way we'll do whatever they tell us. I never thought Papa would scare so easily."

Eliza flew to their father's defence. "The governor wanted to buy Clipper, and Papa wouldn't let him. He talked him out of it."

Jeremy didn't seem to hear her. "That's what is wrong with this country," he fumed. "Everybody's running around scared all the time, letting the redcoats kick us around like dogs!"

Papa and the governor were shaking hands, as though they had completed an agreement. The governor and his men remounted their horses and clattered back to the road. Eliza realised that she hadn't heard the two assistants utter a word. *They weren't there to speak*, she thought. They were simply there to do the royal governor's bidding.

"Papa!" Jeremy cried as soon as their visitors were gone. "Did you really sell one of the teams? Is it true?"

"I sold Maura and her team," Papa said. His voice shook as he added, "I had no choice."

"Of course you had a choice!" Jeremy exploded. "You could have told him no!"

Papa sighed. "It isn't that simple," he said. "In business we have to make compromises."

"Business!" Jeremy repeated scornfully. "It isn't business when we're dealing with bullies. It's coercion."

"Jeremy!" Papa said, and there was a warning note in his voice. "I won't have you speaking that way about the governor. It's disrespectful."

"Jeremy, you've been listening to the wrong people," Ben added fiercely. "A lot of the farmers around here just like to stir up trouble."

"To the British we're nothing but slaves," Jeremy

flashed. "Penn marches in here and orders you to give him a team and a wagon. What more proof do you need?"

"He isn't stealing Maura's team!" Papa exclaimed. "He's buying the horses at a fair price."

"And you're selling them because he threatened you," Jeremy flung back. "You don't have the courage to stand up to him!"

"Jeremy!" Eliza cried, aghast. "Don't talk like that to Papa!"

Jeremy turned away. "I'm sorry," he muttered. "But they can't treat us this way. It isn't right."

The clang of a bell floated across the yard. Rebecca Carter stood at the door, summoning her family in to dinner. Mary scampered ahead to her mother, still chattering about the governor's visit. The rest of them trailed behind, slow and heavy-hearted.

The table was set with wooden trenchers heaped with chicken and potatoes, squash and beans. Papa and Mama sat at either end, facing each other, their four children arranged between them. *Papa looks older this summer*, Eliza thought with a pang. His hair had gray streaks that she hadn't noticed before, and weather and worry had carved deep lines in his forehead and around his eyes. In contrast Mama still looked fresh and young, despite her endless chores. Her hair was still golden and shining, and her blue eyes sparkled with her zest for life.

From the head of the table Papa led the family grace. With her head bowed, Eliza listened to his familiar words, giving thanks for the food that was set before them. They had so many blessings, she thought – health and prosperity, a fine house and land. They worked hard, and they had always been happy.

Over the past year, however, she sensed a creeping change in Jeremy. He worked as hard as ever, but he always seemed to be seething with anger. Sparks flew between him and Ben, and now he even flared up at their papa.

Many people said that the British treated the colonists unfairly and that the local council had no real power. The final word always came from England. Eliza supposed that there was some truth behind all the talk. At one time or another Parliament in London had imposed taxes on everything from glass to tea to playing cards. A year ago colonists in Boston had protested by dumping chests of British tea into the harbour, and Parliament had closed the port of Boston as a punishment. But Boston was three days' journey away, and London lay across the vast Atlantic Ocean.

Why should events in those distant places affect the people of Pennsylvania? Why should her family be torn apart by things that happened in the world outside?

"Amen," Papa said. Eliza looked up with a feeling of guilt. She'd hardly heard a word of Papa's prayer.

"Amen," they all murmured, and their voices merged into one. *This is how we are meant to be*, Eliza thought fervently – seated around a long, laden table, together.

⋆ Chapter Three ⋆

The horses had had their day of rest, and this morning there was plenty of work for them to do. Papa called Ben, Jeremy, and Eliza together in the yard and explained the day's projects. Ben and Jeremy would drive their teams the twelve miles into Philadelphia to deliver flour to merchants on Market Street. On the way home, Ben was to stop at the farm of Jonas Howell and collect a load of grain for the mill.

"And Jeremy," Papa said, his voice steady with resolve, "after you deliver the flour, you'll take Maura and her team to the governor's mansion."

Eliza braced herself for a torrent of outrage from Jeremy, but to her relief he nodded in silence. Perhaps he felt remorseful after yesterday's outburst and had made up his mind to do what Papa asked.

"Eliza," Papa went on, "Luke Pryor is supposed to leave a message for me with Henry Emery at the store. I need you to ride in and pick it up."

Eliza beamed. Henry Emery's store at the little crossroads village of Judsonville served as the gathering place for the local farmers and their families. A visit to Mr Emery meant news, company, and perhaps a peppermint stick as a special treat.

Ben and Jeremy led their teams out of the barn. After promising Clipper that it would be his turn next, Eliza helped put the other horses into harness and hitch them to the wagons. *She and her brothers were like a well-seasoned team of horses,* Eliza thought, *with Papa as their leader.* They had worked together for so long that they hardly needed words – a nod, a raised eyebrow, the sweep of a hand were all that was needed to convey what had to be done.

The horses waited patiently, but the swishing of their tails and the twitching of their ears told Eliza that they were eager to be working again. When they shook their heads, the little bells on their headgear jingled cheerfully. Eliza paused beside Maura and leaned her head against the mare's warm, solid shoulder.

"I'm going to miss you," she murmured. The words could hardly squeeze out past the lump in her throat. She gave the other three horses goodbye pats and hoped they would all be well cared for.

Papa opened the gate, and Hansel's team rumbled out of the yard with Ben in command. Jeremy waited motionless on Zeke – the big bay gelding who served as Maura's left wheelhorse. Eliza watched him closely. His slim body was taut, his face was guarded and vigilant. It was clear that something was not right. Jeremy seemed willing to comply with Papa's wishes, but Eliza sensed that resentment smouldered beneath the surface.

At last the way was clear, and Jeremy picked up the long rein. He leaned down from his high perch on Zeke's back. "Goodbye, Papa," he said. "Good-bye, Eliza. Say goodbye for me to Mama, and Mary, too."

"You're only going to Philadelphia," Eliza said, forcing a laugh. "You sound as if you're heading off on an ocean voyage."

Jeremy did not laugh in return. "Don't worry if I'm late," he said. "I'll be all right."

Eliza felt a knot pull tight somewhere in her chest. "Jeremy—" she began, but at that moment he flicked the reins along Maura's back, and the team surged forward as one. "Goodbye!" Eliza called, and for some reason she found herself adding, "Be careful!" She didn't think Jeremy heard her. Her words were lost in the thud of hooves and the groan of the laden wagon.

"Papa," she said when the wagons had rolled out of sight. "Do you think there's going to be trouble?"

Papa shook his head. "The kind of trouble they're having up in Boston? I doubt it. Pennsylvania's a much quieter place." He paused. "Besides, the King's Regulars are here in case a rebellion breaks out."

"That's good, I suppose," Eliza said, but she didn't feel satisfied. She had been thinking about trouble in the Carter family, not trouble in the Colony of Pennsylvania.

As soon as the wagons had gone, Eliza saddled Clipper, and the two of them set out for the village. Without the weight of the wagon to drag behind him, Clipper seemed to revel in a sense of freedom. He cantered along the road, his head high and proud. Astride his broad back, Eliza carried the reins loosely in her hands and breathed in the late summer fragrance of hay and cornhusks. The day was crisp and cool – a reminder that geese would be flying soon, and winter gales would howl around the doors. But for now, the cornfields rippled with plenty, the sun shone, and the world seemed at peace.

Papa had assured her that there would be no trouble between the British and the people of Pennsylvania, and Eliza trusted his knowledge and experience. Of course some of the farmers were angry that the British had sent troops to control a rebellion here, simply because a few Bostonians had protested against the new taxes. It was a bit unsettling to meet red-coated men with muskets on the roads. Still, the soldiers she had met behaved like gentlemen and clearly meant no harm. The presence of the King's Regulars might even be a boon to colonial farmers and tradesmen. The quartermasters would buy heaping wagons full of corn and flour, dried beef, and live chickens, and the Carter teams would be kept busy hauling supplies to the gates of the garrison. Prosperous days lay ahead, Eliza told herself firmly. There was nothing to fear.

A rabbit darted across the road, almost under Clipper's hooves. A lot of horses would have been startled, but Clipper steadily cantered onward. It wasn't true, what Papa told the governor – Clipper wasn't hard to handle, if you took the time to get to know him. He was everything a horse should be.

The next moment Eliza heard a frantic rustling from

the underbrush on the side of the road. There was a growl and then a few feeble squeaks as the thrashing grew more violent. Then it fell silent.

The rabbit, Eliza thought. Rabbits were abundant at this time of year, and weasels and foxes hunted them night and day. Many would not survive. It was a simple fact of nature — but her heart beat faster, as though she was in danger herself.

At the top of a rise Eliza and Clipper emerged from the woods above the village. Judsonville was a scattering of small wooden houses, an inn, a smithy, and the store, where two horses stood tied to the hitching rail. Eliza knew them both. The roan gelding belonged to John Robinson, one of the farmers who had helped fix Jeremy's broken wheel the other day. The little chestnut horse was Lady Susan, Luke Pryor's prized mare. Eliza would be able to hear Papa's message from Pryor himself.

Eliza slid to the ground. She poured a handful of oats into Clipper's feedbag and tied him to the rail next to Lady Susan. The horses whickered their greetings as Eliza pushed the door open and entered the store.

Along one wall stood barrels of pickles, sweetmeats, salt, flour, and cornmeal. An open bin bristled with nails of assorted sizes and thicknesses. The smells of tobacco and molasses mingled with the scent of the sawdust that Henry Emery sprinkled over the rough floor each morning.

At this time of year no fire glowed in the stove, but three men huddled around it as though it was a blustery morning in December. Henry Emery, a heavy, balding man with warm blue eyes, stepped away from the others to greet Eliza.

"What do you need today, young lady?" he asked. "I have some beautiful oranges – just came in from Spain on the Mermaid."

Eliza stared with longing at the plump, round fruit that he held up for her to admire. She had only tasted an orange once, and she still remembered its startling, sharp flavour, like nothing else in the world.

"Only a shilling," Mr Emery said, "or two of them for one and six."

"I can't," Eliza said, shaking her head. "Why do they have to cost so much?"

"If we could trade with the Spaniards themselves, we could all feast on oranges every day," said John Robinson. His voice was as clear and strong as if he was preaching a sermon. "But under these Intolerable Acts that Parliament has passed, only British ships can bring cargo into our ports — and British merchants charge us what they please."

"That's just the beginning," Mr Emery said. "They can order us to quarter their officers in our own homes, and there isn't a thing we can do about it. And those poor folk up in Boston, with the port blockaded, no goods going in or out — as bad as things are here, it's much worse for them!"

"Is that Eliza?" Luke Pryor exclaimed, holding out a work-hardened hand. "Your papa sent you to look for me — am I right?"

"He did," Eliza told him. "When will your grain be ready?"

"We should have a load ready for the mill tomorrow, if the weather holds."

"Next thing you know, they'll be taxing every trip to the mill," John Robinson went on. "Or they could post a customs agent at each crossroads, charging sixpence per rider."

Eliza stood her ground. She wanted to know what all these mutterings were about. "Why are the Intolerable Acts different from all the other acts before?"

Mr Emery looked surprised, but he answered her. "These acts basically mean that we colonists no longer have any say in our own governance – even our town meetings are run by the British."

"It means that we are nothing but profit to the British," John Robinson added bitterly. "They intend to wring us dry."

Eliza studied a jar of candies, with thoughts filling up her mind. The new British soldiers might benefit her family's business, but surely not having a say in any new laws was too big of a price to pay.

Mr Emery gently changed the subject and offered Eliza one of a fresh bundle of penny peppermint sticks – her favourites. She was searching for a penny in her apron pocket when she heard shouts and hoofbeats outside. Boots stamped in the yard, and two men in British uniforms strode into the store.

One stood by the door, while the other marched up to Mr Emery. "Are you the proprietor?" he demanded.

"I am," Emery said steadily. "Would you care to tell me who you are?"

"We're customs agents for the Port of Philadelphia," the man said. "We're here to certify—"

"I paid my taxes in June," Emery interrupted. "I can show you my receipts."

The customs agent didn't seem to hear him. He

brandished a fistful of papers. "We need an inventory of all your merchandise," he declared. "Show us a list of the imported items you carry."

"A written list?" Mr Emery repeated. "Why? I've already paid!"

"This is outrageous!" John Robinson exclaimed. "You've got no right to harass this man – he's a British subject!"

"We have every right to see his accounts and examine his merchandise," said the agent by the door. "We'll take inventory ourselves."

"Leave this store!" Robinson said fiercely. "You have no right—"

The man by the door called outside. Eliza drew back behind a barrel as more men rushed into the room. She couldn't count them in the blur of movement and couldn't pull words from all the shouting. Someone pried the lid off a barrel in the corner. Someone knocked over a stack of crates. John Robinson lunged for one of the agent's men, but two more caught him by the arms and flung him aside easily.

Instinct told Eliza to run for the door and escape, but she felt that she couldn't leave Mr Emery and the others. It wouldn't be right to flee when her family's friends were in danger. She stood motionless, watching in horror as the scene unfurled before her.

While his men held Robinson and the others at bay, the customs agent went about his business. He yanked open drawers and rifled through their contents. He pawed over bolts of calico. He disappeared into the back storeroom and emerged a few moments later with a smug, satisfied smile. "You owe sixteen shillings more," he announced. "Pay up, and you'll hear no more about it."

Wordlessly Mr Emery counted out the money. The agent took it and wrote out a receipt. "All right," he told his men, "we'll be off." They left the store as swiftly as they had come, and Eliza heard their horses galloping into the distance.

It was astonishing, Eliza thought, *that so much damage could be done in so short a time.* The customs agents had been in the store for less than ten minutes, but they left a shambles in their wake. The floor was littered with nails and papers. A brown river of molasses oozed from an overturned keg. Even the jar of peppermint sticks was broken, its contents trampled into the sawdust.

"How could we let them do this?" Luke Pryor groaned. "We should all be hanged for cowardice."

"You should never have handed over that money,"

John Robinson told Mr Emery. "It'll only encourage them to do this to shopkeepers in other towns."

"I paid today," Emery said, "but the British will pay later on. Our business with them isn't finished."

Eliza bent down and gathered a handful of nails. Her hands were shaking. Nothing made sense. The whole world seemed to have flipped upside down.

"Don't worry, Eliza" Mr Emery said gently. "We'll clean up. Get home to your papa."

"I'll give him your message," she said to Luke Pryor. Her own voice sounded far away.

"Yes," he said vaguely. "Tomorrow."

"I wish you didn't have to see that," Mr Emery told her.

"I wish none of us did," Eliza said.

Outside she found Clipper tugging at the rein, his ears twitching with agitation. "It's all right, fellow," Eliza told him, but she no longer believed it was true.

⋆ Chapter Four ⋆

As soon as they left the village, Eliza spurred Clipper to a gallop, and she found the speed matched her restless mood. They broke away from the road and took the shortcut through the woods and across the Werners' meadow. Clipper scrambled over a dry stream bed and crashed through the underbrush on the far side. The brush thinned and they entered an open woodland of maple and oak. Clipper moved his big body with ease among the tree trunks, and within minutes they reached the wagon yard. Eliza dismounted and quickly rubbed down Clipper before she turned him loose in the pasture. She felt as breathless as if she had run all the way on her own two legs.

"Back so soon?" Mama asked as Eliza entered the kitchen.

For a moment Eliza couldn't answer. Her mother saw the look on her face and rushed forward. "What's wrong?" she demanded. "What happened?"

"Oh, Mama!" Eliza gasped. "They tore up Emery's store! They dumped everything out and made him pay more—"

"Who?" her mother interrupted. "What are you talking about?"

Eliza dropped onto a stool and poured out her story. Her mother listened, shaking her head in dismay. "How dare they!" she exclaimed when Eliza was finished. "Those people in Boston are right – we shouldn't pay British taxes at all if they're going to treat us like this."

"It was terrible," Eliza agreed. "But we have to pay whatever taxes they say – it's the law!"

"We weren't in London when Parliament passed its Intolerable Acts," Mama pointed out. "We had nothing to say about it."

"Papa wouldn't like to hear you say that," Eliza said, glancing around the kitchen.

Mama sighed. "I know. He still feels more British than American. Your grandfather always taught him to

51

be proud of the mother country."

Eliza had never known her Grandfather Carter, who died of a fever when she was only a baby. Papa always spoke of him with admiration – how he'd come to Pennsylvania all the way from Dorset in England, and made his fortune shipping grain and chickens from farms in New Jersey. He had made the most of his life in the colony, but he was a man of England till the day he died.

"I hate to think what Jeremy will say when he hears what happened," Eliza confided. "This will make everything even worse."

Rebecca Carter ran a hand through her hair. "I need to have a talk with Jeremy," she said. "Whatever he thinks, he has to respect his father."

"I thought Papa would get angry yesterday," Eliza said, "but he just looked sad."

"These are sad times," Mama said. She straightened abruptly and put on a determined smile. "Well, we've got chores to do. Go help Gretchen in the parlour."

Gretchen, the German housemaid, was busy with the feather duster when Eliza joined her. Eliza found a rag and began to polish the brass candlesticks on the mantelpiece. The parlour was the most solemn room in the house, its walls hung with Carter family portraits.

Grandfather Carter himself hung by the window and Papa and Mama looked down from above the settee. Ben, in his painting, had a worried expression; Eliza could imagine his restlessness as he sat for the artist, wanting only to get back to his work. There were no pictures yet of Mary, but a portrait of Jeremy and Eliza hung in an honoured spot above the fireplace.

As Gretchen began to sweep the drawing-room, Eliza paused to study their portrait closely. It had been done when she and Jeremy were nine years old. Mr Jonathan West, the painter, had posed them on a bench, their heads bent together over a book. Though Eliza wore a flowered gingham frock and Jeremy wore a boy's short trousers, anyone could see their twinship at a glance. They shared the same reddish-blonde hair, the same slender build, and the same heart-shaped face. The painting captured the sparkle in their eyes and their mischievous grins, as if they'd been whispering secrets – as surely they had.

Mama said that Jeremy and Eliza had invented their own language when they were infants. Now and then one of them would utter a string of mysterious words, and together they would burst into peals of laughter while the rest of the family sat baffled and amazed. Their magic language faded as they grew older, but their deep bond of twinship seemed stronger every year.

If it hadn't been for Jeremy, Eliza might have been trapped at home like most girls her age. Cooking, washing, and mending would have been the substance of her world. But from the beginning, Eliza and Jeremy were a team. Jeremy followed Papa and Ben, learning everything he could about horses and the grain business. Eliza was there beside him, and she learned just as quickly and eagerly as her brother. At first Papa frowned and tried to shoo her into the house, but as soon as her chores were finished she was always out in the stables again. Mama didn't protest, and her silent encouragement wore away Papa's resistance.

When Eliza was seven, Mama sewed her a divided skirt so she could ride astride as the boys did. Eliza and Jeremy learned to ride on a pair of chestnut ponies, Sally and Sammy. Soon they moved on to the big, gentle Conestogas and together they rode through the woods and fields, exploring every yard of the country around Judsonville.

In the past few months, however, Eliza felt a widening distance between Jeremy and herself. He seemed to be drifting away, like a boat that had loosened from its moorings at the dock. Instead of riding with her, Jeremy spent his spare time with his friend Martin, John Robinson's son. Papa said Martin was an agitator, but Jeremy paid no attention. The more time he spent at the Robinsons' farm, the more Jeremy grumbled against the British. Sometimes Eliza thought he didn't care about anything these days except the grievances of the colonists.

If only things could have stayed as they used to be, Eliza thought wistfully as she gazed at the portrait. Life was so simple when they were nine, struggling to sit still while Mr West painted their portrait.

All afternoon Eliza waited anxiously for Ben and Jeremy to return. Every so often she left her chores to peer out the door, straining her ears for the thud of hoofbeats and the creak of wagon wheels. Nothing broke the stillness but the drumming of a woodpecker in the chestnut tree. *Where are my brothers?* Eliza wondered, pacing restlessly from room to room. *They ought to be home by now. What's keeping them?*

Eliza was on her way to bring Clipper in from the pasture when Mary gave a shout. "Here comes Ben! He's all by himself!"

Sure enough, Ben drove Hansel's team into the wagon yard. Jeremy should have been walking alongside, or riding on the lazy board, the wooden seat that folded out from the front of the wagon. But just as Mary said, Ben was alone.

"Where's Jeremy?" Eliza demanded.

"Your guess is as good as mine," said Ben grimly. "He took off somewhere and didn't bother to tell me where he was going!"

"Took off?" repeated Mama, hurrying to join them. "What do you mean?"

Ben told his story as he unhitched the team. He had left Jeremy with the first Market Street merchant and gone on to unload his wagon at a warehouse by the river. When Jeremy's wagon was empty, he was to deliver Maura's team to the governor and walk back to meet Ben for the trip home. "I waited and waited," Ben said. "I looked for him all up and down Market Street. A lot of farmers were in town today. He must have gotten a lift from someone else. But he should have let me know!"

Mama shook her head, troubled. "But he hasn't gotten a lift here. This isn't like him," she said.

"It isn't," Eliza echoed. "It's not like him at all."

Mama served supper late, hoping that Jeremy would be home in time to join them, but night fell and still Jeremy did not come back. Papa paced the drawing-room, frowning. Ben fumed that Jeremy was becoming rude and thoughtless. Eliza exchanged worried glances with her mother. Something was gravely wrong.

Eliza slept fitfully that night. Each time she woke, she remembered with a jolt that Jeremy was not asleep in the boys' room down the hall. Every other night of her life she had known that they were both safe beneath the same roof. Now he was missing. Where had he gone after he delivered the horses to the governor? Perhaps he had been attacked by robbers on the streets of Philadelphia. Maybe he lay beaten and bleeding in some filthy alleyway.

But what had he meant with his parting words: "Don't worry if I'm late. I'll be all right"? Perhaps Jeremy had planned his disappearance all along. What was going on? It wasn't like Jeremy to keep secrets from her.

At first light Eliza slipped downstairs. Papa, Mama and Ben were in the dining-room ahead of her, all looking drawn and tired. Papa and Ben would be going to Luke Pryor's to load his grain harvest. Whatever else happened, the day's work had to be done.

"Papa," Eliza asked as he and Ben were hitching Hansel's team to the wagon, "may I ride into Philadelphia and look for Jeremy?"

Papa stared at her, amazed. "Philadelphia!" he repeated. "By yourself?"

"I've been there enough times with you and the boys," she pointed out. "I can find my way around."

"Philadelphia's not like Judsonville," Papa warned. "It's not a friendly place. And you're a girl – it isn't safe."

"But Jeremy is missing!" Eliza cried. "We've got to do something!"

"Suppose you go missing too," Papa said, shaking his head. "Then we'll have two of you to worry about!"

"I'll be all right; I'll take Clipper," Eliza said. "If I leave right away we can be back by dark. You and Ben won't have time to go until tomorrow. If Jeremy's in trouble, we can't make him wait that long!"

"Where will you go?" Papa asked. Eliza thought "will" was a good sign, as though he had made up his mind to let her go.

"I'll talk to people at the market, ask if anyone has seen him. And I'll stop at the Red Rooster Tavern. You always say that the woman who runs it – Mrs Manders – knows everything that happens in the city."

Papa thought for a moment. "All right," he said at last. "We need to start somewhere. Go and learn whatever you can. But be careful! And hurry back!"

Clipper was cheerful company as they left Judsonville

behind and cantered along the open road. His bridle jingled as he tossed his mane, his nostrils flared to take in the scents of hay and moist earth. On an ordinary day Eliza would have delighted in the long ride. She was thrilled that Papa trusted her to carry out her mission. Yet her mind kept returning to worries about Jeremy, and she scarcely noticed the late-summer morning.

The noise of the city reached her even before Philadelphia rose into sight. She heard the shouts of carters, the rumbling of wagon wheels, and the clop of horses' hooves on the cobblestone streets. Street vendors called out their wares: buckles and ribbons, newspapers, candles and pies. The city closed in around her, busy and uncaring. Rows of brick houses crowded along both sides of the narrow streets. Eliza reined Clipper to a walk, and he manoeuvred doggedly among the carts and carriages that clogged the way.

"I don't like it any more than you do," Eliza told him. "The city makes me feel like a twig in a forest."

In Judsonville everyone knew her and her family, but here no one cared who she was or where she came from. She was glad that Clipper towered above most of the other horses around them. Perched high on his back she could see beyond the tumult around her, and take in the city's wider scope. Off to her right a street ran down to the river lined with docks. Ahead gleamed a limestone church front, crowned by a sparkling steeple. In the distance, frowning down from the top of a hill, she could see the chimneys of the governor's mansion.

Eliza was about to turn Clipper toward Front Street and the Red Rooster Tavern when a cartload of squawking chickens rumbled into their path. A cart wheel jammed on a stone, and the driver cursed and clambered into the street to see what had to be done. The cart completely blocked the entrance to the street, and so Eliza had no choice but to let Clipper continue on in the direction of the church.

Again Eliza looked up at the governor's mansion. Someone there – a groom or stable hand, or even the governor himself – had seen Jeremy when he delivered the team and the wagon. Perhaps they could tell her if he said anything about where he planned to go next.

I can go back to Mrs Manders later, Eliza decided. The governor's mansion would be her first destination.

The streets grew less congested as Clipper climbed the hill, and his pace quickened to a trot. A pair of armed soldiers stood guard at the gates to the mansion grounds. They bowed slightly, to acknowledge that they were in the presence of a young lady.

"What brings you to His Excellency's mansion?" the guard on the left demanded.

Eliza remembered the uniformed customs agents at Henry Emery's store, and felt a tightness in her chest. *Don't look afraid*, she told herself sternly. *Look as though you have every right to be here!*

"I'm here on business," she said, glad again for Clipper's extra height.

"If you're trying to sell something, go around to the back gate," the guard told her. "The cook will see you."

"I have business with Governor Penn," Eliza said. She made her voice sound bold, though she was shivering inside.

"The governor doesn't do business with wenches from the country," the guard on the left put in with a sneer.

Clipper stamped impatiently, and Eliza patted his neck. His presence somehow gave her courage. "My father, Abraham Carter, sent me," she stated. "The governor himself came to see us the day before yesterday."

The guards looked at each other and shrugged. The one on the left pointed to a hitching post. Eliza dismounted and looped Clipper's reins through the post's iron ring. All alone she started up the flagstone walk to the mansion's broad stone steps.

A maid in a starched white apron met Eliza at the front door. She hesitated when Eliza said she had come on an errand to the governor. The housekeeper was called in, and the two of them conferred in low voices while Eliza waited in the echoing, high-ceilinged vestibule. At last the housekeeper turned to her and beckoned her to follow.

"You can wait in the library," she said through tight lips. "The governor is very busy. I hope you are not wasting his time."

The governor's library was a stiff, formal room, shelves of leather-bound books lining the walls on two sides. In the corner stood a massive roll-top desk, tightly shut to conceal its contents. A tall, wooden clock presided opposite the cold fireplace. Eliza perched on the edge of a chair and watched the clock's pendulum sweep back and forth, back and forth, counting away the minutes. Now that she was here, what was she going to say to Governor Penn? Probably the governor had no idea of her brother's whereabouts. But she had to begin her search somewhere. She had to find out everything she could.

At the sound of footsteps in the hall she sprang to her

feet. Governor Penn strode into the room, talking to someone over his shoulder. When he caught sight of Eliza he stepped back in surprise.

"Miss Carter!" he exclaimed. "To what do I owe this honour?"

Eliza curtseyed. "My father sent me to see you," she said. "He hopes you are well."

"Very well, thank you," the governor said curtly. "I'd have thought your father would send one of your brothers."

"My brothers," she repeated, confused. "Ben is working today, and Jeremy – we don't know—"

"I wouldn't expect a young lady like you to drive a team and one of those big wagons all the way into Philadelphia by herself," the governor said, shaking his head. "But I'm glad you're here, at any rate. Your father promised the horses would be delivered yesterday. By this morning I was starting to wonder."

What was he saying? Eliza let his words run through her mind again, trying to seize their meaning. The governor was still waiting for the horses! That meant they hadn't arrived yesterday. Jeremy had never brought them to the governor's mansion at all!

What had happened? What had Jeremy done?

⋆ Chapter Five ⋆

*P*rotect *Jeremy!* The thought flooded Eliza's mind, washing away every other concern. If for some reason Jeremy had chosen not to deliver the horses, Eliza mustn't let the governor grow suspicious. Papa had sold the horses to the governor; they belonged to him now by right. If Jeremy had taken them somewhere else the governor could say he had stolen the team. Under the laws of the Crown, horse-thieves could be hanged!

There was no time to devise a plan. Eliza pounced on the first story that popped into her mind.

"Papa sent me to tell you he meant to deliver the team yesterday," she said. "But Maura cast a shoe, and now she's favouring her right foreleg. Papa wants to wait till she's better."

Governor Penn frowned. "This is very important!" he fumed. "I need the team right away. Your father gave me his word!"

"I know," Eliza said apologetically. "He said to tell you how sorry he is. Only he'd never deliver a team that's not in perfect condition."

"How much longer will it be?" the governor demanded.

"Tomorrow, we hope," Eliza assured him. "If Maura's doing all right."

"Thank you," the governor told her. "And thank your father for me. Mrs Simmons will show you out." The governor gestured toward the door to let Eliza know that she was dismissed. He barely seemed to notice her curtsey of farewell.

Out in the hall Mrs Simmons was on duty, ready to escort her to the front door. Eliza raced down the flagstone path to the gate, where Clipper stood waiting. She unhitched him from the post, glad to be near him as her mind raced, and led him through the gate past the stone-faced soldiers. In moments she was in the saddle and galloping back down the hill.

All her life Eliza had understood Jeremy's thoughts and

feelings. Now, as she left the mansion behind her, she felt a growing certainty that Jeremy had never intended to bring Maura's team to the governor. He loved the horses and he couldn't bear to see them in service to the Redcoats. But where would he hide them?

Eliza thought carefully. Jeremy wouldn't keep them in Philadelphia, with its dirty, thronging streets. They would need wide fields for grazing and running. He'd want to keep them safe, somewhere familiar, somewhere close to Judsonville.

She'd be wasting her time if she went to Mrs Manders, Eliza realised. Once his load of flour was delivered, Jeremy would have gotten the horses out of Philadelphia as quickly as he could. He would turn homeward, back to the country he knew so well.

As they neared the foot of the hill the street grew more crowded, and Clipper slowed to a walk again. They threaded their way among the carts and peddlers, the sound of Clipper's hooves drowned by the noise around them. Papa said that some thirty thousand people lived in Philadelphia.

Why do they all choose to live crammed into a city, Eliza wondered. Wouldn't any reasonable person prefer the open air of the country instead? It didn't make sense –

but not much was making sense to her these days.

When they emerged at last onto the open road, Eliza nudged Clipper to a fast canter. They glided past fields and woodlands, devouring the miles.

What should I do now? fretted Eliza. She knew she ought to go home and tell Papa and Mama. Papa had sent her to gather information, and she owed him a report on what she had learned. But her news would throw her parents into an agony of worry. It would be far better, she decided, if she tried to find Jeremy herself and persuaded him to deliver the team tomorrow. As long as he came home tonight and took the team to Governor Penn in the morning, all would surely be forgiven. She would search the route home for signs of the team.

At every bend in the road Eliza peered into the woods, half expecting to see a big Conestoga head gazing back at her. The woods stretched on endlessly, west all the way to the Ohio country. They held countless thickets and hollows where horses could be hidden away. Even huge Conestogas could be tucked out of sight in the Pennsylvania forests. She and Jeremy were at home in the woods around Judsonville, as much as any fox or deer. If Jeremy was determined to conceal the horses, he knew dozens of places where no one would find them. How would she ever find him?

Eliza could try to outguess her brother, but time was critical. It would be far easier if she could talk to someone who knew Jeremy and was aware of his plans. Martin Robinson would be a good source of information, but the Robinson farm lay six miles off the road, deep in the forest. The Werners' farm was much closer, Jeremy might have stopped there.

Over the years Eliza had visited her friend Harriet Werner so often that she knew and loved her whole family. Jeremy loved the Werners too. Eliza remembered how he had welcomed Mr Werner's help when his wagon was broken down in the stream. Maybe he had gone to Mr Werner and confided his plans for the horses.

Eliza turned Clipper off the road, and they cut across the fields to the Werners' farm house. Old Peter Beekman, baling hay behind the barn, glanced up as she passed. Peter had no land of his own, and hired on wherever he found work. Some people said Peter was shiftless and lazy – that if only he'd worked hard, he'd have something to show for it.

He's certainly working hard now, Eliza thought, as she watched him twist together the thick, prickly bundles of hay. Though his body was bent, his arms were muscled and strong.

"You here to see Harriet?" Beekman inquired. "She's on the front steps with her mother."

"Thanks," Eliza called over her shoulder.

Just as Peter said, she found Harriet and her mother, Margaret Werner, sitting in the shade on their front steps, a sewing basket between them.

"Hello!" she called as she dismounted. "I'm on my way home from Philadelphia, so I thought I'd stop by."

Harriet sprang up from the step, her chestnut brown curls bouncing up and down. She was small and quick as a sparrow, with a sparrow's bright, inquisitive eyes. "I'm so glad to see you!" she exclaimed. "It's been so long since we've had company! Everyone is busy this time of year."

Mrs Werner, her dark hair in a tight bun, slid over on the step and made room for Eliza to sit down. "How are your mother and father?" she asked. "And Mary – is she staying out of mischief?"

"Sometimes," Eliza said. "Last week she found a litter of kittens in the barn, and brought them all into the house. Mama found them mewing in the clothes hamper."

"Cats are fine in their place," Mrs Werner said,

nodding, "and their place is in the barn."

"I had a letter from Susan Howe," Harriet announced. "It's four pages long!"

"How did she fill up four whole pages?" Eliza marvelled. "I never heard her say more than three words at school."

Eliza listened patiently as Harriet chattered about Susan and her news. They'd been out of school since May, and Harriet, who was an only child, was clearly lonesome. At last, when the topic wound down, Eliza asked casually, "You haven't seen my brother Jeremy by any chance, have you?"

Beside her, Harriet stiffened and glanced away. Margaret Werner cleared her throat. "No," she said abruptly. "We haven't seen him since church last Sunday."

Eliza looked at Mrs Werner in surprise. Her smile had vanished. Her lips were thin and tight, and her gaze veered away.

Eliza tried again. "I just thought to ask, because—"

"We don't know where your brother is," Mrs Werner interrupted. "I'm sorry we can't help you."

"Mr Werner might know something," Eliza persisted. "May I ask him?"

There was a short pause. Harriet and her mother

shifted uncomfortably, and Harriet grew very intent on the sewing in her lap. "My husband isn't at home," Mrs Werner said at last. "I don't know when he'll be back."

Abruptly Mrs Werner got to her feet. "I have to check my bread," she said. "It should have risen by now. Harriet, I need you to help me."

On any other day, they would have invited Eliza inside. She'd have helped with the bread-baking while they talked and laughed together in the kitchen. But today was different. Harriet gathered up the sewing and rose, looking down at her feet. Her mother hurried into the house without a backward glance.

"Is something wrong?" Eliza asked. "Are you angry with me?"

"No, of course not!" Harriet said, and for a moment her eyes brimmed with tears. "It's just that – so much is going on, it's not safe for anyone any more."

"Is your family in trouble?" Eliza asked in alarm.

Harriet shook her head. "If I could tell anyone, I'd tell you," she said fervently. "But I can't talk about it. I need to go now."

Impulsively Eliza gave her friend a parting hug. "Come see me as soon as you can," she said. "Please!"

"I will," Harriet promised. "When all this is over."

With a deep sense of foreboding, Eliza mounted Clipper again and headed back toward the road.

"What secret are the Werners hiding?" she said aloud to Clipper, who whinnied as if to say he couldn't tell. "It has to be something important, to make them act so strangely."

Eliza was so distracted that she rode straight past Peter Beekman without noticing him again. Suddenly she heard his voice behind her, calling her back. "Miss Eliza! I need to have a word with you!"

Startled, Eliza swung Clipper around. The old man looked taller than she remembered, and his face was stern. "Does your father know what your brother Jeremy is up to?" he asked.

Eliza had the chilling sensation that Peter was peering into her mind. A shiver ran through her, and Clipper edged back a step in response. "What are you talking about?" she demanded. "What do you know about my brother?"

"I see things," Peter said smugly. "I hear things when people don't think I'm listening."

Eliza twisted the reins in her hands. "Do you know where Jeremy is right now?"

Peter's face contorted with bitterness. "He's with the

rest of the rebels, hatching a plot against His Majesty."

"Rebels?" Eliza repeated. The word sounded like sharp stones grating together.

"They'll hang for treason, the whole pack of them," Peter said with grim satisfaction. "And your brother too, unless your father takes him in hand."

"Just tell me where I can find him!" Eliza pleaded.

"The Robinson place! They're up to something out there," Peter declared. "Tell your father! Your father had better bring that boy home before it's too late!"

"Thank you!" Eliza cried. She turned Clipper back toward the road. Behind her, Peter Beekman warned, "It's treason! They'll all hang for treason against His Majesty!"

⋆ Chapter Six ⋆

Eliza knew a shortcut through the woods beyond the Werners' back pasture. But it would be rough going on horseback, through underbrush and clumps of dense tree trunks, and finally across a steep ravine. So, though the distance was longer, she decided to take the Judsonville Road instead.

After a mile of riding she reached the trail that branched to the Robinson farm. In places the trail was so faint that it nearly disappeared. It was just what Eliza expected from John Robinson. He was a man to go his own way, not caring much for other people's opinions. It seemed entirely fitting that he had settled his family on a remote farm in the deep woods where no one was likely to interfere with him.

Eliza longed to hurry, but she let Clipper choose his own pace along the uneven ground. Sometimes he carried her at a slow walk, picking his way among rocks and tangled underbrush, and it was a relief whenever they reached an open stretch and Clipper broke into a canter that devoured the distance.

She had promised Papa that she would hurry home from the city. She'd assured him she would be back before dark. Now it was almost nightfall, and she still hadn't found Jeremy. *I have to find him and the horses before I go home*, Eliza thought. She had to bring them back tonight, so he could deliver the horses to Governor Penn in the morning!

A brown-and-white dog barked as they approached the Robinson farmhouse. In a frenzy of yapping it darted between Clipper's hooves. As usual Clipper held steady, ignoring the dog as he would a whining mosquito. Eliza dismounted and fastened Clipper's reins to a tree limb. The door of the house opened, and John Robinson's wife Jennie stepped outside. She was a pale, weary woman with a sad face. She looked Eliza over, frowning.

"Oh, it's you," she said, clearly displeased by what she

saw. "Did your father send you?"

"No," Eliza said. "I'm looking for my brother."

"He isn't here," Jennie Robinson said with a sigh. "John and Martin are gone too. I'm by myself with the little ones."

As she spoke, the ringing of iron on iron broke out somewhere behind the house. Jennie Robinson's face went red and she covered her mouth with her hand.

"It sounds like somebody's back there," Eliza said. "What's all that noise?"

"Oh – it's nothing," Mrs Robinson stammered. "My little ones – they're always up to some mischief. If I see your brother…" She broke off and rushed to stop Eliza as she headed around the corner of the house to investigate. Eliza pushed past her and kept walking. She was tired of being lied to. It was time for her to uncover the truth.

In the first moment Eliza saw only an ordinary barnyard. A few hens scratched in the dirt, and a cow lowed a greeting, hoping to be milked. The barn door stood wide, and Eliza saw the broad side of a familiar blue Conestoga wagon.

In the next moment she noticed the smoke – a thick, acrid cloud rising from somewhere behind the barn.

The clanging grew louder. The murmur of male voices rose and sank like the blows of the hammer.

"Nearly done," someone said.

Someone answered, "An hour yet till sundown..."

Eliza froze. That was Jeremy's voice – so familiar, so beloved, and somehow so wrong emerging from the woods behind the Robinsons' barn.

Eliza didn't give herself time to think. "Jeremy!" she cried, rushing forward. "Jeremy! What are you doing here?"

Jeremy stood beside the fire, dipping something into a white-hot pan with a pair of tongs. Half a dozen other boys and men were busy around him. Some tended the fire. Rudolf Werner hoisted a heavy sack and headed toward the barn.

"Eliza?" Jeremy said in disbelief. "How did you find me?"

"Never mind that!" Eliza exclaimed. "Where are the horses?"

Jeremy didn't answer. He shifted the tongs, refusing to meet her gaze.

"You didn't take Maura's team to the governor!" Eliza said accusingly. "What did you do with them?"

"Don't ask questions," Jeremy said. "Just go home.

Forget you were here, all right?"

Eliza faced him squarely, hands on her hips. "I'm not going home unless you come with me!" she stated.

"Settle down now!" Rudolf Werner told her. His voice was coaxing, as though he were talking to a fractious horse.

Eliza paid him no attention. "Jeremy, listen!" she plunged on. "You promised Papa you'd deliver the team. You promised!"

Mr Werner set down his sack. Everyone turned to stare. "Come on, Eliza," Jeremy pleaded. He put his hand on her arm and tried to lead her away from the others.

Eliza planted her feet and refused to budge. "Where are the horses?" she repeated. "Are they here?"

Jeremy was silent. Eliza jerked her arm free and marched into the barn. Just as she'd suspected, the big blue wagon bore the name CARTER DISTRIBUTION COMPANY along one side in bold white letters. Maura leaned her dun-coloured head over the door to the first stall and watched Eliza with her soft, gentle eyes. The rest of the team was there, too – Cricket, Annie, and Zeke. She was relieved to see them.

"They're some of the best horses in the colonies," Jeremy said coldly behind her. "I couldn't just hand them over to the Redcoats!"

"But they don't belong to us any more!" Eliza spun around. "Papa sold them to the governor. You've stolen them!"

"Papa sold because he was afraid," Jeremy shot back. "The governor has no right to threaten people just because he works for the Crown!"

"Governor Penn can have you tried for horse-stealing! He can have you hanged!"

Jeremy fell silent again. He looked down at the straw-strewn floor.

"I did what I could to protect you," Eliza said. "I told the governor Maura came up lame yesterday. I said Papa wants to wait till she's all right again."

"You talked to the governor?" Jeremy asked, amazed.

"I rode in this morning to look for you. I found out you never delivered the team."

"You rode to Philadelphia all alone?" Jeremy exclaimed. "Papa let you go?"

"He's worried about you," Eliza said. "We all are. We were afraid something terrible had happened when you didn't come home."

"I said not to worry about me," Jeremy reminded her. "When I said goodbye – remember?"

"Don't you know how serious this is?" Eliza burst out. "I had to lie! I had to lie to the Governor of Pennsylvania! He thinks you're going to bring the team as soon as Maura's leg is healed."

"Well, it looks like she's incurable," Jeremy declared. "Nobody will ever make me take the team to the governor. Not you, not Papa, not anybody!"

"What's going on? Need some help?" John Robinson stood in the doorway, his son Martin by his side. Rudolf Werner edged in behind them. They regarded Eliza with suspicion.

Jeremy stepped protectively between Eliza and the others. "I'm just talking to my sister," he said. "It's all right."

"What's she doing here?" Martin demanded. He was a slightly-built boy of seventeen with a keen, intelligent face. Now he watched Eliza narrowly from beneath his thatch of thick sandy hair.

Eliza felt the depth of their mistrust. It gave her a strange, shrinking feeling inside. She fought to hold her ground. "I came with a message for Jeremy," she said. "Our father needs him at home."

"We know all about your father," Rudolf Werner said, in his faintly accented speech. "You tell your father to mind his own business!"

Eliza hoped Jeremy would leap to Papa's defence, but he said nothing. "The Loyalists don't care about anything but making money and kneeling to the king," John Robinson said sourly. "We're all free men here."

Eliza turned and paced across the barn. She wanted to be away from John Robinson and the others, far from their sneers and half-veiled accusations. Papa hadn't done anything wrong! *They* were the rebels, these men gathered in secret at John Robinson's farm, hiding the stolen wagon and Maura's team. Eliza didn't know what they were scheming to do. She only knew that Jeremy was here with them, and she had to bring him away.

What drew Jeremy to this place and these wary, secretive men? They shared his fierce anger at British treatment of the colonists, and she had seen for herself the British at their worst. She remembered the customs agent rifling through drawers and flinging goods from shelves while Mr Emery watched in helpless rage. The colonists deserved respect. They should be treated fairly. Nevertheless, loyalty to the governor and the king was part of life. That was the way it had always been, and always would be.

At the barn door, Jeremy and the others were deep in talk. They spoke in low voices so that she couldn't hear their words. They were discussing her, she knew, and telling each other that she was uninvited and unwelcome. She couldn't be surprised by such behaviour from the Robinsons, but how could Mr Werner treat her so shabbily? Once he had joked that she was his second daughter – but now that ease and friendliness seemed forgotten.

What really mattered, though, was Jeremy. Her own twin, the person she had always loved and trusted so deeply, was pushing her away as if she were a stranger. Jeremy acted as though his rebel friends meant more to him than his own family! He didn't seem to care what trouble he stirred up between Papa and the governor. He didn't even mind risking his neck to the hangman's noose.

Eliza paced back toward the row of stalls. Looking up to watch Maura, she accidentally brushed a heap of sacking with her foot as she passed. There was a sharp, metallic clink, and she glanced down quickly. Her foot had kicked loose a corner of the sacking. Peeking from underneath was the gleaming barrel of a musket.

"Get away from there!" John Robinson shouted, lunging toward her. "What are you doing, snooping around?"

Arms! Of course! It all made sense now. They were

gathering weapons and forging ammunition. Jeremy and his companions were preparing for an armed uprising!

"She's a spy!" Martin yelled. "We should have chased her away the minute we saw her!"

"What do we do with her now?" Rudolf Werner asked, glaring at her. "If we let her go, she runs straight to her Loyalist father and tells him everything!"

For the first time, Jeremy spoke. His voice was clear and calm, and filled with certainty. "Abraham Carter is my father too, and I'm still one of you. You can count on my sister not to say a word about what she's seen here. She's no more a spy than I am."

★ Chapter Seven ★

"How can we be sure?" John Robinson demanded. "We can't afford to take chances."

"You have my word," Jeremy said. He looked at Eliza, and she knew she had to speak for herself.

She drew a long, quavering breath. "I promise," she said slowly, "I won't tell anyone what I've seen today."

"Not even your dear Loyalist father?" Martin said, with his usual sneer.

Eliza flashed Jeremy an imploring glance. Did he really expect her to keep a secret from their own father?

Jeremy's look was clear and unwavering. Without words, Eliza read his meaning. "Not even Papa," she said slowly. "You can count on me."

The men shrugged, accepting her promise warily. Martin Robinson watched her with eyes as hard as granite chips. "You better mean what you say," he told her. "We won't forget."

With the question of Eliza settled, the men went about their business once more. The Robinson farm, tucked deep in the woods, was as busy as an anthill. Eliza counted a dozen men, some she recognised and others who were new to her. Some men melted lead and moulded musketballs. Others loaded barrels of powder into the governor's wagon. No one talked much, but Eliza sensed a spirit of urgency and excitement about their activities. They were preparing for a confrontation, and they seemed eager for whatever would come.

"I need to get home," Eliza told Jeremy as he piled sacks in a corner of the barn. "What should I tell them?"

"You can't go now," Jeremy told her. "It's almost dark. You'll have to wait till morning."

The sun had begun to sink behind the treetops, and Eliza shuddered at the thought of taking the trail in the dark. Still she insisted, "Clipper can find the way. I've got to go – Papa and Mama will be worried!"

"There are wolves in these woods," Jeremy reminded

her. "Snakes and sinkholes. Wait till tomorrow, when it's light."

Eliza thought she'd rather brave the wolves and snakes than pass a night here at the farm with the rebels, but she held her tongue. "I suppose you're right," she said. "Maybe they'll figure I'm at the Werners' with Harriet."

Jeremy nodded, relieved. As he resumed his work, Martin Robinson came up beside them. He glared at Eliza. "If you're going to stay with us, make yourself useful," he told her.

Eliza stiffened. She wasn't about to take orders from Martin Robinson or anyone else in this rebel band. "First I'll bring my own horse inside," she told him. "Then I'll see to the others and the stable. I want to keep these horses healthy."

The brown-and-white dog dashed in yapping circles as Eliza untied Clipper and led him to the barn. Two little Robinson girls trailed after her, eyeing her curiously. They must be used to seeing strange men who appeared and vanished without explanation. A female visitor – a girl of fourteen – was altogether different. The children couldn't stop staring and whispering behind their hands.

When Clipper was settled in an empty stall, Eliza turned her attention to Maura and her team. There was comfort in familiar tasks, performed in the care of these great, beautiful animals. She raked out their stalls and laid down fresh, sweet-smelling straw. She checked hooves, brushed coats, and filled mangers with hay. She could almost pretend that they were all safe at home again, not marooned here at this hidden arsenal.

When she left the barn, she found that the men had shut down the forge for the night. Their focus had turned from arms to food. A fire roared in the barnyard, and a slab of venison sizzled on a spit. Eliza didn't think she was hungry, but the aroma of roasting meat kindled her appetite. Jennie Robinson bustled out of the house, carrying a basket of fruit and a round loaf of bread. Eliza offered her help, and Jennie smiled at her for the first time. "They're letting you stay?" she asked, her eyebrows raised in surprise.

"For tonight," Eliza said, and followed her into the kitchen to bring out more food.

They ate under a canopy of evening stars. Eliza sat to the side, listening to the talk as it ebbed and flowed around her. A bearded farmer named Rodney Pringle boasted about his harvest, the biggest crop he'd ever brought in. Everyone agreed it had been a good summer.

"Well, it won't help us. It will only make the British rich," John Robinson stated. "They'll never give us a fair price at the market."

"The price always does go down when the grain harvest is good," Pringle pointed out. "We'll still come out ahead."

"Don't be so sure," John Robinson told him. "The British merchants at the market pay us as little as they can, and charge double to the people who come to buy."

Broad-shouldered Abel Grimsby spoke up. "They're getting ready to shut down the port. They want to blockade Philadelphia the way they blockaded Boston. No goods coming in or going out."

"They still haven't forgiven the colonies for that little tea party up in Boston," said Martin. "They should be grateful it was a peaceful protest. People threw a few chests of tea overboard rather than pay taxes on it, that's all."

Martin's father nodded in the firelight. "But it hurt their British pride," he said. "And their pocketbooks! That's why they're sending more troops – they want to bring us to our knees."

After they had eaten their supper, some of the men

took out pipes and tobacco. Jeremy went to work carving a powder-horn from the horn of a cow. The talk flowed on.

"My sister Ellen married a Boston man," Abel Grimsby said. "I have a letter from her. They have six British officers quartered at their house."

"They have no choice, under the law," Martin said bitterly. "Any of us can be forced to do the same."

Jeremy spoke up for the first time. "It will happen, too. All these Redcoats on the way – they'll want to live in comfort."

"They keep my sister running day and night," Grimsby said. "Fetching water, washing linen, polishing their boots – she's a servant in her own home!"

Eliza shuddered. Suppose British soldiers were quartered at her house some day! She imagined their heavy boots on the stairs, their gruff voices bellowing orders. She pictured Mama heating water for their baths and slaughtering the chickens to provide their meals. Her home wouldn't be her own any longer. Men like the customs agents would push her and her family into the corners.

"If it can happen in Massachusetts, Pennsylvania isn't safe," John Robinson said. "But when trouble comes, we'll be ready!"

The others murmured in agreement. "They'll be sorry if they try their tricks on us!" Rudolf Werner put in.

"With the meeting coming up, things will get more serious," John Robinson declared. "Men from all of the colonies are coming to Philadelphia to talk about the situation. If the council can't get through to the governor, the meeting will make him listen."

Eliza leaned forward. What meeting was he talking about? The colonies stretched for hundreds of miles – from New Hampshire to Georgia. For men to travel such distances, something important had to be going on!

"Jeremy," she whispered, "what sort of meeting is it?"

"They call it a congress," he whispered back. "A continental congress."

Continental. Eliza turned the word over thoughtfully. It sounded very big and powerful. It stretched far beyond Philadelphia, beyond Boston even, to embrace the whole string of colonies that lay along the shores of the Atlantic.

"Then His Majesty will sit up and take notice," Martin said. "He'll have to think twice before he tries to collect any more taxes from us!"

"We're free men!" John Robinson said proudly.

"Nobody on the other side of the ocean is going to tell us what to do!"

Rodney Pringle had been listening quietly, but now he spoke up. "Perhaps if they'd give us a voice in Parliament, we could avoid trouble," he said. "We need a voice — a vote."

"We've said that for years," Grimsby said. "But they're not interested in a peaceful solution. It's too late now."

"We'll fight for our rights!" John Robinson said staunchly. "It's time for us to stand up!"

"We'll fight!" the others echoed. "We're not afraid to fight!"

After a while the men spread their blankets on the ground to prepare for sleep. Jennie Robinson invited Eliza to share a room with her girls, Evie and Abigail.

"Thank you," Eliza told her. "I'd be glad to. I'll check on my horse, and then I'll come in."

Clipper whinnied as soon as he heard Eliza's step. He shifted in his stall and reached his head over the door to nuzzle her shoulder. He looked calm and content, unruffled by his new surroundings and the events of the long day.

Eliza entered the stall and leaned her head against Clipper's warm, solid flank. He was so steady and reliable! On the hardest roads she always knew she could trust him. They were travelling a new kind of road now, she thought – a confusing and frightening one.

She had known some of these farmers all her life. They had always been peaceful men. They cared about their fields and crops, and didn't pay much attention to news from anywhere further than Philadelphia. Now everything had changed. They talked about Parliament, about laws and taxes, about a continental congress. They gathered guns and powder.

"It's terrible, Clipper!" she said miserably. "How can they think about killing and dying? What good can ever come from that? And Jeremy's in the middle of it all!"

Clipper turned his head and cocked his ears, taking in her anguished words. In his sympathetic company she found that she had more to say.

"But the British mean to use force to control us," she said. "Why else are they sending soldiers over here? We haven't done anything to deserve that. It isn't right!"

Clipper gave a short, emphatic snort. He seemed to agree completely.

Eliza's thoughts raced on. "If a wolf attacks us, we shoot it to protect ourselves," she said. "If the king's soldiers fire on us, we have to defend ourselves by shooting back."

Maybe it was too late for peaceful solutions, just as John Robinson claimed. Maybe there would have to be bloodshed before the colonies and the mother country settled their differences.

Eliza gave Clipper a final pat and swung the door of the stall shut. One by one she checked on the other horses. She was glad they wouldn't be going to Governor Penn after all. She was glad they wouldn't haul supplies for the soldiers who came to fight the farmers of Pennsylvania.

⋆ Chapter Eight ⋆

Eliza woke with the feeling that a weight pressed on her feet.

"Get off!" someone whispered. "Don't bother her!" When she opened her eyes she discovered six-year-old Evie sitting at the end of the bed, while her older sister Abigail tugged at her arm. They both grinned when they saw that she was awake.

The children's smiles were so open and welcoming that Eliza couldn't quite believe the events of the day before. The upstairs room at the Robinson farmhouse, with the sun streaming through the east-facing window, filled her with a sense of well-being. Perhaps nothing was as grim as she had imagined. Maybe she could persuade Jeremy to go home today after all.

Down in the kitchen Jennie Robinson was making breakfast for the children. She urged Eliza to join them, but Eliza shook her head. "I have to go," she said. "My father will be out looking for me."

Jennie nodded and handed her a biscuit. Eliza thanked her and munched it hastily as she hurried out to find Jeremy.

The men were already up and busy. They had rekindled the forge and were waiting for it to grow hot. Yesterday's musketballs had cooled, and Jeremy and Martin were dropping them into deerskin pouches.

"I'm leaving now," Eliza said. "Jeremy, please – come home with me."

Jeremy looked up, frowning. Beside him Martin Robinson speared her with his cold, hard glance. "We went through this yesterday," Jeremy said. "I can't go home. You know that."

His face was impassive, but Eliza wouldn't give up. "Well, I can't go without you!" she protested. "What would I say to Papa?"

"You're not going to say anything, remember?" Martin put in. "You gave us your word."

Eliza tried not to listen. In the freshness of morning

she wanted to believe that Jeremy would hear reason.

"Tell Papa you couldn't find me," Jeremy said firmly. "That's all you can do right now."

"What about the horses? What should I tell him about them?"

"You didn't find the horses either," Jeremy said. "You don't know anything."

"Oh, Jeremy!" she groaned. "It isn't right to hide from your own family! We should all be together!"

Jeremy's eyes grew sad. "I know," he said in a low voice. "I wish it didn't have to be this way."

All of the brightness seeped out of the day. Resigned, Eliza saddled Clipper and led him out of the barn. She mounted from a tree stump and gathered up the reins. "Take good care of Maura and the team," she told Jeremy. She hesitated and added, "Stay out of danger."

"I don't know if I can," Jeremy told her. "We'll do our best to protect each other."

Clipper seemed to sense Eliza's heavy heart. His gait was slow and measured, as though he were hauling a wagon filled with grain instead of bearing one slender rider on his back. Eliza did not try to hurry him away from the farm. She knew Mama and Papa must be frantic with worry by now, but she dreaded having to face them. How could she pretend that she knew nothing of Jeremy's whereabouts? Lying to Governor Penn was bad enough, but deceiving her own father and mother was unthinkable.

Nevertheless, she had given Jeremy her word. She couldn't go back on her promise. Jeremy believed he was doing the right thing, for himself and his family and for the whole Commonwealth of Pennsylvania. If the British really threatened to harm honest, hardworking farmers and shopkeepers, people like Henry Emery, something surely had to be done. Maybe Jeremy was foolish to put his safety at risk, but he was brave, too. He was unshakeably committed to the path he had chosen, and Eliza found herself admiring his determination.

Clipper's pace quickened as they took the turnoff that led to the Carters' wagon yard. "Eliza's here!" Mary shouted. She had posted herself as lookout in the branches of an oak tree that stretched above the road. She scrambled down and raced off to spread the word.

Papa rushed to the gate. "Eliza!" he cried. "You're safe! Thank God!"

"I'm sorry I couldn't get home last night," she said, reining Clipper to a halt. "It got too late to travel."

Ben emerged from the barn, wiping his hands on his

trousers. "So, where were you?" he asked. "Wasn't it bad enough everyone worrying about Jeremy? Did you have to disappear too?"

Papa frowned at him and tried to soften what he had said. "Your mother was sure you were at the Werners'. She kept warning us not to let our imaginations run wild."

Eliza felt a flicker of relief. If Papa believed she'd been with Harriet last night, there was no need to lie outright.

"I'm sorry you worried," she said, swinging out of the saddle.

Her feet had barely touched the ground when Papa asked, "Do you have any news about Jeremy?"

For just an instant she hesitated. Whether he approved or not, Papa deserved to know the truth. If only she could tell him the whole story!

She shook her head. "No," she said simply. "Nothing."

"Where did you go?" Ben demanded. "Who did you talk to?"

"I went all the way to Philadelphia. I talked to some of the farmers from around here, too." Every word was true, she thought. She hadn't invented a bit of it.

Papa and Ben followed her as she led Clipper into the barn. They helped her unsaddle him and rub him down. "Who did you see in the city?" Papa asked. "Did you talk to Mrs Manders?"

"Not exactly," Eliza admitted. "I didn't go down there."

"Well, where *did* you go then?" Ben asked.

There was no way around it. She would have to describe her visit with Governor Penn. Anyway, the governor was bound to send a message complaining that the team hadn't been delivered. She needed to give fair warning. "I went to the governor's mansion," she explained. "I wanted to trace where Jeremy had been, so I thought I should make sure he delivered Maura and the team."

"And did he?" Papa asked apprehensively.

Eliza tried to steady her voice. "No," she said. "Jeremy never brought the horses there."

Papa's face went white. "Are you sure?" he asked.

Eliza nodded. "I saw the governor. He told me himself."

"What could have stopped him?" Papa exclaimed. "There must have been an accident!"

Ben slammed a fist into his palm. "It wasn't any accident," he said furiously. "He didn't want to take the team to the governor so he's gone off with them somewhere."

"He couldn't do that," Papa protested. "He wouldn't!"

Ben was adamant. "He's going to ruin the business and he doesn't care," he said. "The way he's going, he'll get us all hanged!"

Papa sank onto an upended barrel, his head in his hands. "My own son," he said in a ragged voice. "I never thought one of my own boys would betray me!"

"He didn't betray you," Eliza insisted. "We don't know yet what happened. We don't know why – "

"It's theft," Ben said bluntly. "Maura's team belongs to the governor now."

"Did he pay for them?" Eliza asked.

"Not yet," Papa said, "but we shook hands. I'm bound by a gentleman's agreement."

Eliza hung Clipper's saddle on its peg. She forked hay into his manger and gave him a parting pat.

"The Carter Distribution Company will be ruined," Ben declared. "Count on the governor to see to that."

"The business is the least of it," Papa said. "We're talking about your brother – "

"My brother the rebel!" Ben broke in. "That's where he is, you know – he's off somewhere with his rebel friends."

Papa didn't try to argue with him. He seemed very old and tired. "No matter what he's done," he said,

"Jeremy is still part of this family. None of us should forget that."

The simple words wrapped Eliza like a goose-down comforter. Whatever happened, Papa wouldn't cast Jeremy aside.

"What did you say to the governor?" Ben wanted to know.

"I told him Maura's limping. I said we can't deliver the team until we're sure she's all right."

For the first time Papa's face showed a glimmer of hope. "If we can put Penn off for another day or two," he said, "we still might find Jeremy.

"Maybe he'll send word to us," Eliza added. "It'll turn out all right somehow."

"Well, let's go talk to your mother," Papa said. "She'll be glad to know you're back."

They were heading for the house when hoofbeats sounded on the road. *Jeremy!* Eliza thought with a leap of joy. He had changed his mind. He was bringing the team home after all.

In the next instant, Eliza's hope shrivelled and died. Flanked by a pair of red-coated British soldiers, Governor Penn rode into the yard. Papa threw Eliza a look of panic. "Maura's foreleg," she whispered. If she could lie to the governor, maybe Papa could do it too.

"Good morning, Your Excellency!" Papa called. "I hope you're well."

"I'm in fine health, Carter," the governor said gruffly. "I hope the same is true for that dun mare you sold to me."

With a sickening jolt, Eliza realised they had come to a decisive moment. Everything depended on Papa's answer. She held her breath, waiting.

"Maura?" Papa said. He gave a regretful sigh. "She's improving, but I'll have to wait another day or two."

Eliza didn't dare look at Papa. Any fleeting glance between them could rouse the governor's suspicions. "I haven't got a day or two!" he snapped. "I need a team right away!"

"Tomorrow then," Papa said. "If Maura's not ready, I'll send one of our other teams."

"I'll take that big black gelding with the white blaze on his forehead," Penn stated. "He was my first choice to begin with."

"Clipper?" Papa asked. "He's a very strong leader. The whole team is outstanding."

Eliza gasped. How could Papa offer Clipper so casually, as though he were any ordinary horse? Clipper was hers! She had trained him herself. He knew her commands, her touch, her moods – sometimes he even seemed to know the thoughts that streamed through her head. How could Papa think of selling him?

"Clipper is hard to handle!" she exclaimed. "You have to ride him or he won't listen – "

"Eliza!" Papa said sharply. "This is a matter of business!"

The governor ignored Eliza's outburst. "Tomorrow then," he said. "By the way, if all goes well, Simon Billings will make arrangements with you to haul his grain in the next few days."

"It's arranged already," Papa said coolly. "We pick up his grain this afternoon."

Eliza saw to her satisfaction that the governor looked taken aback. He couldn't threaten to take away Billings' business any longer. But Penn recovered quickly, and turned his attention to Ben. "This is your older son, isn't it?" he asked Papa. Without waiting for a reply he added, "How's that other boy of yours? The younger one."

"Jeremy?" Papa said, startled.

"Jeremy. That's it. How is he these days?"

A prickle of fear crawled up Eliza's spine. Governor Penn's question was casual, as if he and Jeremy were old friends. But the governor had scarcely met Jeremy until he came to buy Maura's team the other day. An unspoken meaning lurked behind his words – a meaning and a threat.

"Jeremy's doing very well, thank you," Papa said. "It's kind of you to ask."

"He's a fine young man," Governor Penn remarked. "He has a great future ahead of him. These days, some young fellows veer off course. But I'm sure you won't let your boy be led astray."

The governor wheeled his horse, and the soldiers followed with precision. The three horses moved in unison, like a well-trained team. Without a backward glance the riders headed out to the road.

"Now look where Jeremy's rebel friends have gotten him!" Ben exploded. "If he'd just stayed home none of this would be happening!"

"I don't like this," Papa said, shaking his head. "The governor taking an interest in Jeremy all of a sudden – I don't like it at all."

"Neither do I," Eliza said. The governor suspected something. Maybe he had heard that Jeremy was working with the rebels. Perhaps he would send some of his soldiers to find Jeremy and bring him back to be questioned.

If only she could tell Papa the truth, Eliza thought in

anguish. Together they could decide what to do. But she had given her word not to reveal what she knew. "Maybe the governor is looking for Jeremy too," she said. "We have to find him first."

"I hope we can," Papa sighed. "I hope we can!"

✶ Chapter Nine ✶

Mama had been in the spring-house, churning butter with Gretchen. But Mary had pulled her away from in the cool wooden shack over the river, to pour out all of the news. "And Governor Penn," she was saying, "he wants to buy Clipper if he can't get Maura. That means we'll have only one team left!"

Mama looked up, her eyes questioning as they approached. "It's true," Papa said. In a few sentences he described the governor's visit. "Jeremy never delivered Maura's team," he concluded. "Eliza couldn't find him anywhere."

"Let's just hope the British can't find him either," Mama said. "The governor won't take this lightly."

"Ben and I are going out to look this morning," Papa said. "I'll talk to people in Judsonville. Ben, you try the farms out toward Delaware Ridge."

"What about Simon Billings?" Ben asked. "We can't just put our work aside."

"Work will have to wait," Papa said sternly. "Your brother comes first."

"Why don't you take Mary with you?" Mama suggested. "She'd love a trip into town."

"Yes! Yes! Yes!" Mary cried, bouncing up and down. "Can I go, Papa?"

"Well, all right," Papa said after a moment's thought. "You can ride pillion with me on Brutus."

"Maybe I'll be the one to spot Jeremy," Mary said gleefully. "I'll keep a sharp lookout!"

Guiltily Eliza watched them make ready for the search. She could save everyone so much trouble, she thought. If she chose to, she could lead Ben and Papa straight to Jeremy. Surely Jeremy would go home if Papa ordered him to do so.

The image of Martin Robinson pushed its way into her mind. She remembered the sneer in Martin's voice when he said *dear Loyalist father*. She remembered the way he warned her to keep their secret, and his promise that he wouldn't forget if she broke her word. Papa might not be safe if he visited the rebel camp. The men out there had plenty of firearms and ammunition. How far would they go to protect their hideout? They had trusted her to some extent, but Papa might be in danger.

"Eliza and I will finish the churning," Mama told Gretchen as the horses clattered out to the road. "Go and see if the washing is dry."

Gretchen nodded and slipped away. Eliza wondered what she thought about the Carters and all their turmoil. Gretchen didn't ask questions or offer opinions. She simply did her work and stayed away from trouble.

That's how her family had always lived too, Eliza thought. As the people around them muttered about taxes and injustice, the Carter wagons rolled on. There were orders to collect, receipts to sign, deliveries to be made. Until today. Today, for the first time in Eliza's memory, Papa had set work aside for a more important purpose.

"How are the Werners?" Mama asked when they were alone.

Eliza thought of the strange, stiff scene on the Werners' front steps. "They seem to be fine," she said carefully. She knew she ought to add details, but nothing sprang to mind.

"How is Harriet?" Mama tried again.

"She misses our friends from school," Eliza said. "I think she's lonesome sometimes."

"Do you ever feel lonesome?" Mama asked.

Eliza pondered. "Not really. I get to travel all over, helping with the teams. I see lots of people. And I have Clipper—" Her voice wavered, and she couldn't go on.

"And now the governor wants to buy him," Mama said gently. "Of course you're unhappy about that!"

"We could sell Hansel's team instead," Eliza said, fighting back her tears. "Why does it have to be Clipper?"

"The governor chose him," Mama pointed out. "After Maura, Papa can't afford to offend the governor a second time."

Eliza took Gretchen's place at the churn. Her thoughts were far away as she turned the crank around and around. She imagined Clipper hauling supplies for the Redcoats at the garrison. Would he ever have a chance to run in open fields, to graze freely on meadow grass and clover? Would anyone love him and care for him and braid his forelock with pompoms? Would anyone understand that Clipper had to be ridden as lead horse, and treated with kindness and respect?

"Eliza," Mama said suddenly. "I have to ask you a question."

Eliza tensed. "What is it?" she asked.

Mama gave her a penetrating look. "How much do you know about what Jeremy's doing?"

"What makes you think I know anything?" Eliza asked, stalling for time.

"I know how close you two are," Mama said. "Even if Jeremy doesn't confide in you right now, you'll make it your business to find out what's going on."

Eliza weighed out her words. She couldn't evade her mother's question, but she needed to guard Jeremy's secret. "I know he's with some people who are angry at the British," she said.

Mama nodded. "I'm not surprised. But do you know where he is?"

Eliza stopped churning, but her fingers stayed locked around the handle. It hadn't been very hard to lie to Papa, she realised, because Papa would rather not know about Jeremy's involvement with the rebels. Mama was different. She was determined to learn the truth.

"I saw him," she said at last. "I talked to him. But I

can't tell you where he is."

"He may need our help!" Mama protested. "We have to be able to reach him."

Eliza shook her head. "I can't tell anyone," she said. "I promised."

Mama watched her intently. She gave a long sigh. "All right," she said. "I won't press you. At least he's safe for now."

"He is," Eliza assured her. "For now, anyway."

"It breaks my heart, that we've come to this," Mama said. "Trouble with the British has been building for a long time, but I never thought it would tear our family apart."

"I keep wishing Jeremy would stay away from it," Eliza told her.

"I think it's too late for that," Mama said. "Unless Parliament changes direction, I'm afraid we're all headed for war."

War. The word landed between them with an ugly thud. It had hung over the countryside for months, dreaded and unspoken. People talked of 'resistance,' of 'fighting back,' as though one or two skirmishes would set everything right. But war? War meant hunger, destruction, and death. Death for many, on both sides.

"Can't we do something to stop it?" Eliza pleaded.

Mama shook her head. "It's out of our hands," she said. "All we can do now is pray that it's over quickly."

"But how can war solve anything?" Eliza asked. "It will make everything so much worse!"

"It will," Mama agreed. "But maybe in the end the colonies will become independent. Some day maybe people will feel the war was worth fighting."

How can any war be worth fighting? Eliza wondered. People would kill. People would die. Would Jeremy raise his musket and take the life of another human being? She couldn't bear to think of her gentle brother committing such a cruel act.

Then an even more frightening possibility assailed her. Would Jeremy himself be struck down by some red-coated British soldier? The very thought gave her an aching sense of emptiness. How would she live if Jeremy were gone from the world?

"I don't see how anything can make war into a good idea," Eliza said.

She resumed her churning, and for a while they were quiet. There was no sound but the rhythmic thump of the churn and the bubbling of the spring nearby. By now Ben and Papa were well on their way, asking for news of

Jeremy from everyone they met. She alone knew his secret. She was the only one of them who could find him and warn him that the governor was on his trail.

At last Eliza broke the silence. "Mama," she said, "as soon as I finish churning I need to see Jeremy. I have to tell him that the governor knows he's with the rebels."

"Don't worry about chores," Mama said. "Go right now."

By daylight the path out to the Robinson farm was easy to trace through the woods. Clipper remembered the way, and stepped smoothly over rocks and woodchuck holes. Here and there Eliza spotted his hoofprints from their earlier visits, cut like small buckets into the soft earth.

They had nearly reached the farm when the report of a musket ripped the stillness. Clipper shivered and came to an abrupt halt. Eliza's heart raced. In an instant she guessed what had happened. The governor and his men had found the rebels' hideout! They had crept through the woods and surrounded the farm. She was too late to warn Jeremy. At this very moment he was caught up in a battle to the death!

Another shot rang out, and a third. Then a light breeze sprang up, carrying with it the sound of voices and laughter. "Bull's-eye!" someone yelled. "Try to beat that!"

"Come on, Clipper!" Eliza said, relieved. "It's only target practice!" Steady as ever, Clipper set off again. When the next musket fired he only twitched his ears and kept walking.

The brown-and-white dog greeted them with its usual yapping. Eliza ignored it and rode around to the back of the house, where she found John Robinson conducting a lesson on marksmanship with Martin and Jeremy. A target, the roughly-drawn form of a British officer, had been nailed to the side of the barn. The bull's-eye was painted in the middle of the soldier's chest.

Martin Robinson sighted along the barrel of his musket. "Hold her a little lower," his father cautioned. "There… you've got it. Now, let him have it!"

The powder flashed, but this time there was no sound of a shot. Martin kicked a tree root in disgust. "You've got to be more patient," John Robinson said. "Make sure your powder's really caught before you pull the trigger."

Jeremy turned at the sound of the horse and hurried over to Eliza, swinging his musket. "Why did you come back here?" he demanded. "You're going to give us away with all your riding back and forth!"

"Jeremy, listen!" she said. "This is important. The

governor stopped by this morning. He asked Papa about you."

Jeremy shrugged. "And?"

"Isn't that enough? It means he's thinking about you, paying attention to what you're doing. Jeremy, I think he knows you've run off to join the rebels!"

"Maybe it'll help him wake up," Jeremy said. "We're ready to fight back, and he may as well know it."

"I'm serious!" Eliza cried. "There will be soldiers looking for you. They'll arrest you for treason."

Jeremy patted his musket fondly. "If they come for us, we're ready for them."

"Ben and Papa are searching all over, trying to warn you!" Eliza said. "Mama's worried sick!"

"You didn't tell them where I am, did you?" he asked in alarm.

Tears stung Eliza's eyes. "That's all that matters to you now! You don't care about us any more! Your own family – don't we even count?"

"*I do care!*" Jeremy said fervently. "That's why I'm here! I'll fight for my family if I have to. I'll fight for our country. No king off in London is going to tell us how to live!"

Eliza looked at him imploringly. She saw the resolve

in his face, and the strain of tiredness, anxiety and fear. There was compassion, too. It pained him to break away from his family this way, yet he felt he had made the only possible choice.

"Nothing will change your mind," Eliza said in resignation. "But Jeremy, please – be careful. Be on the lookout."

Jeremy gazed at the men and boys scattered around the yard. "We will," he said. "I promise you that."

Eliza wheeled Clipper around and headed back down the path. The woods swallowed the sounds of target practice, and birds twittered and rustled as though nothing were amiss. As they approached the foot of the path Eliza saw a shadow looming on the road. It was a lone horseman, sitting motionless. When she drew closer, she saw that the horse was Hansel, and the rider was her brother Ben.

For a long, taut moment their eyes met. Ben's gaze seemed cold and knowing. It chilled Eliza to the bone. Then, without a word of greeting, Ben urged Hansel forward and cantered away up the road.

✶ Chapter Ten ✶

It was a good thing that Clipper knew the way home. Eliza sat in the saddle, her mind reeling, too dazed to give him commands. She let him take full charge, and he set off at a brisk walk.

What was Ben doing, waiting at the beginning of the path to the Robinson farm? Why didn't he speak when he saw her? She could reach only one conclusion – Ben had been spying on her. He suspected she knew where Jeremy was hiding, and he had determined to find out for sure.

If only she'd been more careful! She should have made sure no one was following her, that no one was watching from the woods beside the road. In fact, she shouldn't have gone to talk to Jeremy in the first place. Her visit hadn't accomplished anything, and now Ben knew Jeremy's whereabouts. It was as if she'd broken her promise and told him the whole story herself. Jeremy would feel betrayed. How could he ever forgive her?

Papa and Mary were back from Judsonville when Eliza rode into the wagon yard. From the slump of his shoulders she saw that Papa had no news. *Will Ben tell him what he's learned?* she wondered. Where had he been heading when he cantered away in his stony silence? Maybe he intended to share what he knew with the governor's men!

Eliza braced herself to be pounded with questions about why she had gone out and where she had been, but Papa seemed too distracted to wonder. "I hope Ben is having more luck than I did," he said, pacing the yard. "Nobody in town would admit to knowing a thing. They're hiding something. I could see it in their faces. They know more than they'll tell."

"I got a bag of sweetmeats," Mary piped up from beside the woodpile.

"I'm going out again," Papa said. "I'll talk to the Howells and the Schmidts." He paused, looking at Eliza as though he hadn't quite seen her before. "Since Ben isn't here, you'll need to pick up the grain from Simon Billings."

"With Clipper?" she asked, startled. "He's already had a ride today. He should rest up."

"I have no other team to send," Papa said with a spark of impatience. "Ben is out on Hansel. It's an easy haul to the Billings place with the empty wagon. Clipper can rest while they're loading."

"I wish we didn't have to do business with anyone in the governor's family!" Eliza's words caught her by surprise. She hadn't known they were about to fly out of her mouth.

"Never mind what you want or don't want," Papa said sternly. "We need to keep the governor happy for as long as we can. Maybe he'll forget about hunting for Jeremy."

"I hadn't looked at it that way," she said. "If it could help Jeremy, of course I'll go."

"Thank you," Papa said. "I'll be off as soon as I talk to your mother."

With Mary sprinting before him, Papa headed for the house. Eliza led Zeus, April, and Tillie into the yard and began harnessing the team to the empty wagon. She had the wheel horses secure between the shafts when Ben rode quietly into the yard. Calmly he dismounted and led Hansel toward the barn.

"Hello, Eliza," he said over his shoulder. "Where are you off to?"

For a moment Eliza stood speechless. He acted so casual, as if nothing strange and sinister had happened between them. Was she supposed to pretend she hadn't seen him by the Robinson path?

Eliza flung down Tillie's harness and rushed toward her brother. "I saw you!" she exclaimed. "You were waiting there on the road."

Ben nodded. "There were hoofprints," he told her. "Big Conestoga prints. I thought maybe they were Maura's." He hesitated and added, "Or Clipper's."

"Why did you just sit there?" she demanded. "What were you waiting for?"

"What do you think?" Ben said sharply. "I was trying to find Jeremy. I saw those prints and I thought he and his friends might be out at the Robinson place. Was I supposed to ride up there into an armed camp? They might have blown my head off!"

Eliza had lied to Papa and the governor. Lying to Ben was easy. "Well, Jeremy isn't there," she declared. "I asked Martin Robinson if he'd seen him, and Martin said no."

"If you knew where Jeremy was, I'm probably the last person you'd tell," Ben said ruefully. "The two of you always stick together."

Eliza's hands began to shake. She gripped them hard behind her back, hoping Ben wouldn't notice. "I wouldn't tell you," she agreed, "because I can't trust you. You'd report your own brother to the British, wouldn't you?"

"And what if I did?" Ben shot back. "He deserves to be arrested! Just because a few farmers have grievances he thinks we should start killing British soldiers. Those soldiers are here to protect us!"

"Protect us!" Eliza cried. "I saw what the tax agents did in Emery's store! The British don't care about protecting us, believe me!"

"You're even starting to sound like him," Ben said, scowling.

"And you," Eliza cried, "you sound like a British officer yourself! How can you side with them against your own family?"

"Stop this! Both of you!"

Eliza hadn't heard Papa's approach. Now he stood beside the wagon, and the look on his face chilled her like a January gale. She had never seen him so shaken with fury.

"I won't stand for this!" Papa went on. "I won't have

the two of you slashing at each other like a couple of barn cats!"

Eliza looked at the ground. A stream of ants glided past her feet.

"I'm trying to get her to see reason," Ben began.

"You're both Carters, and don't ever forget it!" Papa cut in. "We're a family. We're loyal to one another first of all."

"Tell that to Jeremy," Ben said boldly. "I think he forgot."

Papa stepped toward Ben, menacingly. Ben shrank back, abashed. "Don't speak to me in that tone again," Papa said with ice in his voice. "We will treat each other with respect."

Ben, too, looked at the ground. "Yes, sir," he said softly. "I'm sorry."

Papa's voice softened too. "Come with me to look for Jeremy," he said. "Eliza will pick up the order from Simon Billings."

Ben nodded, and Eliza felt her tension ease. As long as Papa had an eye on him, Ben couldn't run to the British with news of Jeremy. She picked up Tillie's harness and resumed her work. Last of all she harnessed Clipper into his lead position. She fitted all four horses with their headgears and bells. The cheery jingling seemed starkly out of place today. Still, she reminded herself, she had to uphold the Carter name, and do her part for the Carter Distribution Company.

The empty wagon bounced and rattled merrily along the road, but Eliza felt weighed down with trouble. She was sorry she had added to Papa's worries by arguing with Ben. Still, the things Ben had said were unbearable. He was a threat to Jeremy. But, she admitted to herself, in some ways Ben was right. Jeremy's actions put the whole family at risk. In his own way, Ben wanted to do what was right for everyone's protection – just like Jeremy.

Simon Billings and his three brawny sons must have heard the jingle of the Conestoga bells. They were waiting when Eliza drove the big blue wagon into the grain yard, and they set to work at once. As they hauled the heavy grain sacks and hoisted them into the wagon bed, Eliza unhitched the horses. It could take hours to load the wagon properly, and the team needed a good rest before the heavy haul ahead.

After she had tended to Clipper and the others, Eliza had nothing to do but watch and wait. The Billings boys – David, Noah and Simon Junior laughed and jostled each other as they worked. Once, Noah stuck out his foot and nearly sent David sprawling. Simon Junior roared with laughter, and after a moment even David joined in, as if he had enjoyed the joke as much as the others. They all worked hard, but they saw the afternoon as a chance to have fun as well.

It had been months since Ben and Jeremy had teased and joked with such ease. The mounting tension had robbed them of their old playfulness. When they worked together now, they shared only one purpose – to get the job done.

When the wagon was almost full Simon Senior emerged from the house and announced that the boys could take a break. A maidservant brought out bread and cheese and mugs of ale, and the boys lounged in the shade. "What's your name, Carter girl?" Noah called.

"Eliza," she said, edging away from them.

"Are you hungry, Eliza Carter? Come sit with us!"

"Don't sit with him! Sit with me!" called Simon Junior, laughing. "I'm better-looking, don't you think?"

Eliza felt her face grow hot. She was usually shy around boys she didn't know – and these were the governor's nephews. It would be best for her to keep her distance.

"I'll stay over here, thanks," she said. She felt a pang of hunger as she watched them eat, but she wasn't about to let them know it.

"Give her time to make up her mind," Noah said. "She's trying to decide which of us she likes most."

They were all handsome boys, and Eliza couldn't quite ignore the fact. Of the three of them she liked David the best. He was quieter than his brothers, a watcher and a listener. Once she saw him looking up at the sky, pensive and still, as though he saw pictures in the clouds.

The boys turned away, but Eliza sensed that they were still competing for her attention. They talked about hunting. Simon Junior said it would be pigeon season soon, and Noah boasted that last fall he'd killed twenty-seven birds in a single morning. The flocks had been so dense you could knock birds out of the air with a stick.

"Saves on powder," Simon Junior said. "That way we'll have more to use on the rebels."

Eliza winced. She listened more intently.

"There won't be any rebels left after tonight," Noah said, grinning.

"What do you mean?" David wanted to know. "Is there going to be a fight?"

"Not a fight, no. Papa says they're going to burn out the whole rebel den." Simon Junior spoke with satisfaction. He threw a sidelong glanced toward Eliza, as though he wanted to gauge her reaction.

Maybe they are just trying to impress me, Eliza thought desperately. *Maybe they're exaggerating*. But in the next moment, all her hope vanished.

"Some local has just brought word to the garrison," Noah said. "A gang of rebels is hiding out at a farm in the woods. We finally know where it is."

⋆ Chapter Eleven ⋆

In a few minutes more, the boys went back to loading the wagon. Eliza watched their rough teasing in an agony of impatience. Every moment's delay might cost Jeremy his life. She had to warn him and the others! They were no longer safe at the Robinson farm. At nightfall British soldiers would be on the march.

How could they know? Who would have turned them in? Some local... No one knew of the hideout, except her and... Ben! *Oh no!*

Could Ben have really carried word to the garrison? He had told her that Jeremy deserved to be arrested. Maybe that was his plan – but the British weren't interested in taking prisoners. They wanted to burn the farm. Their plan was deadly destruction.

"That ought to do it," Simon Junior said, thumping the last sack of grain onto the pile in the wagon. "What do you say, Eliza?"

Eliza walked the length of the wagon and studied the load with a practised eye. "This one needs to shift over a foot or so," she said, pointing to one of the sacks. "Otherwise the balance will be off."

"She's not only pretty, she's clever, too," Noah remarked.

Eliza had no time for their games. "And over here," she said. "The one on top has to come down."

Following her directions, the boys rearranged the sacks until the load was distributed evenly. Eliza hitched up the team and mounted Clipper in his lead position. At the first touch of her heels he moved forward, and the rest of the team fell instantly into step. The wagon gave a lurch and began to move. Eliza glanced back to assure herself that everything was in order, and saw David Billings watching her. There was admiration in his gaze. He waved, and she waved back.

"Goodbye!" she called, and set off along the Judsonville road.

Don't think about Ben, Eliza told herself as the wagon rumbled along. But she couldn't put her pain and anger aside. She recalled the look Ben had given her on the road, and he had ridden off in the direction of the city. She had told him that Jeremy wasn't at the farm, but he must have realised the truth. There was no other explanation.

Ben had to have gone to the garrison this morning. Who else could have told the British about the Robinson farm? How could Ben do this to his own brother? Didn't he have a drop of family loyalty?

Eliza shoved thoughts of Ben into a back corner of her mind. Right now she needed to make a plan. She would have to warn the farmers. There wasn't enough time to haul the wagon all the way home, and taking it up the track to the Robinson place would be almost impossible. She needed to leave the wagon somewhere safe, along with April, Zeus and Tillie. On their own, she and Clipper could move fast, and speed was what mattered now.

Where could she leave the team and the wagon loaded with Simon Billings' grain? She had to find a place where the horses would be cared for, and where no one would ask questions. She considered the farms along the road — the Pryors and the McLaughlins, and ruled them out. No, she thought, there was only one farm where she could count on people to help her. She would leave the wagon and team with the Werners.

"Haw!" she cried as they reached the turnoff to the Werners' house and barn. Clipper turned his head, looking back at her in surprise. She had ridden him to the Werner place countless times, but never before with a loaded wagon in tow!

"It's all right, boy," she told him. "We're doing things a little differently today. Haw!"

This time Clipper made the turn without hesitation. For a moment the wagon leaned perilously to the left, and Eliza gasped in dismay. This was no time to overturn in the road! To her relief the wagon righted itself, and rumbled its way behind the team up the Werners' lane.

Harriet and her mother had just brought the cows in from pasture. They stared in amazement as the wagon lumbered toward them, drawn by the full team of Conestogas, heads high and bells jingling.

"Eliza!" Harriet cried. "What are you doing here?"

Immediately Mrs Werner sensed that Eliza's arrival was a sign of trouble. "What's wrong?" she called. "Has something happened?"

"No," Eliza said, pulling the team to a halt. "But it

is about to. I have to ride Clipper out to the Robinson place."

Mrs Werner and Harriet exchanged startled glances. "Why?" Harriet asked in a quavering voice.

"The British are on their way," Eliza said, springing down from Clipper's back. "Help me unhitch the team!"

Harriet and her mother sprang into action. Only yesterday they had tried so hard to conceal the truth from her, but so much had happened since that awkward visit. Now it was obvious that she understood everything, and the Werners no longer had a secret to protect. Without questions they left the cows mooing and pawing, and pitched in to help her. They had no experience with big Conestoga horses, but they were more than eager to do what they could. With two extra pairs of willing hands Eliza unhitched the team in record time. She remounted Clipper and wheeled him around.

"How did the British find out?" Mrs Werner asked. "How do they know about the farm?"

Eliza couldn't bear to tell her. She couldn't admit out loud that Ben had turned his own brother in. Once again she felt forced into a lie. "I don't know," she said. "Someone must have told them."

"Papa's out there," Harriet said, choking back a sob.

"So is Jeremy," Eliza said. "I'm going to warn them, so they'll have time to get away." *Will they?* she wondered. *Can I get to the farm in time?*

"I'll take the shortcut," Eliza added, "through your back pasture."

The Werners had two pastures, separated by a brook. At this time of year the brook was almost dry, and Clipper stepped easily from one bank to the other. The back pasture, as the Werners called it, ranged uphill until it met the woods. By riding through a quarter mile of closely packed tree trunks and crossing a steep ravine, Eliza knew she could reach the path just two miles below the Robinson farm. It would be a difficult ride, but it would save valuable time.

One step after another, she told herself as the dark woods closed around them. Clipper picked his way cautiously, searching out footholds he couldn't see in the tangled undergrowth. His big body crashed through bushes and vines, tearing a path where none had ever existed. Once he came to a full halt before a cluster of trees so dense that he had to take a long detour. Eliza guided him as well as she could, but soon she lost her own sense of direction. Maybe it had been a terrible mistake to come this way! She didn't have time to get lost!

At the top of a ridge Clipper came to a halt again. The foliage was thinner here, and when Eliza looked down, she could see that the ravine lay almost at Clipper's feet. She gave a gasp of surprise and delight. They weren't lost after all! Once they crossed the ravine the Robinsons' path was only a few yards further.

Then she took a closer look at the ravine, and her delight turned to dismay. It looked as though a giant had carved a long, jagged scar into the land with a monstrous knife. She had forgotten that the sides were so steep, and that it was such a long way to the bottom. Years ago she and Harriet had scrambled down one side and up the other on a berry-picking expedition, but she had never attempted to cross on horseback. Now, all too clearly, she understood why.

Clipper drew back, away from the edge. All of his massive power gathered into an unshakeable resistance. He had behaved this way two years ago, Eliza thought, whenever he was hitched to the wagon in the wheel or swing positions. Something within him said, "I cannot. I will not!" and there was no way to persuade him.

It's different now, she reminded herself. She and Clipper had worked together day after day for two years. They knew and trusted each other. Perhaps they could find the way together.

"It will be all right," she told him. "We're going to do this somehow."

Eliza dismounted and walked along the rim of the ravine until she found a place where the grade was not quite so steep. The bottom was some ten feet below her, and halfway down lay a ledge about three feet wide. Even here, it would be a difficult manoeuvre. If Clipper slipped and fell he could break a leg. By choosing the shortcut she had put his life in danger.

But she was endangering Jeremy's life with every moment that slipped away. She couldn't turn back now and take the long way around. They had come this far – they had to go forward.

"Come on, Clipper," she said softly, laying her hand on his neck. "We'll go slowly. You can do it."

Sliding her hand to Clipper's shoulder, Eliza took her first careful step downward. She eased herself to a footing on the ravine's side and gave Clipper a gentle nudge. "Come on," she said, filling her voice with encouragement. "Come with me, Clipper!"

For a moment more, she felt Clipper holding back, resisting with every fibre. Then something in him seemed to yield. He lifted his right forefoot and took a tentative step. One front hoof found a resting place, then the other. He hung miraculously to the ravine wall, tilted at an impossible angle. With a twist in her stomach Eliza saw that it wasn't going to work. Clipper was too tall. His balance was wrong. Inevitably he would topple and fall.

Suddenly she heard Mary's voice inside her head. *Can you teach a horse to sit up or roll over like a dog?*

"Clipper," she whispered, "you can't do it standing. You have to sit and slide."

She knew he couldn't understand her words, and no knowledge of the gestures that could show him what to do. She concentrated on the picture in her mind – the image of the big black Conestoga crouched on his haunches – and pressed down on Clipper's flank. She willed Clipper to understand what she meant.

Clipper's legs flailed wildly. Eliza sprang out of the way, afraid she would accidentally be struck by a flying hoof. Clipper was trying to climb backwards to the rim again, but he couldn't gain purchase on the slippery ground. Instead of climbing up he began to slide downward. "Sit down!" Eliza pleaded. "Down! Down!"

Clipper's rear legs folded beneath him. Twigs snapped, stones grated and tumbled, and the giant horse skidded toward the bottom. The ledge slowed his progress for a moment, but nothing could stop him now. Downward he plunged, forelegs splayed to keep his balance, until he came to rest on the floor of the ravine at last and rose once more to his full height.

Eliza scrambled down to stand by his side. Clipper was blowing and stamping, but she saw at once that he was unhurt. She had never before known that a horse could look amazed. Clipper wore an expression that spoke of pure astonishment.

"Good boy!" she cried, hugging his neck. "I knew you could do it!"

The forest drifted into twilight. There was no time to lavish Clipper with praise; it was almost dark. Eliza picked up the reins and led him up the far side of the ravine. The slope was much more gradual, and it was an easy climb to the top. On level ground once more they made their way to the path that led to the Robinson farm.

The sun was sinking fast, but Clipper moved with complete confidence now. After the ordeal of the ravine, the path seemed easy and familiar. Clipper behaved as though he had memorized every jutting rock and crumbling log. Eliza longed to hurry, but she knew it was wise to let him choose his own pace. The woods loomed deep and quiet. They were alone on the path, and there was no sound or sign of the soldiers.

As she rounded the final bend and the farm came into sight, Eliza saw a reddish glow and a thick smoky haze. For a terrifying instant she was sure that the British had arrived after all, and set the place ablaze. Then, to her relief, she realised she was seeing the glow of the forge at the end of another long day. The house stood solid and certain, with the big red barn planted firmly behind it. The brown-and-white dog yapped his frantic welcome, and Evie and Abigail dashed out to see who had come.

"Will you look who's back again!" Martin Robinson sneered when Eliza rode up to the forge.

Jeremy looked mortified. "I told you this morning!" he began. "What are you doing back—"

Eliza held up her hand to silence them. "You have to listen to me," she said fiercely. "The British are coming tonight. They're going to set the whole place on fire."

"How would you know?" Martin demanded.

"I heard it at the Billings' place," Eliza explained. "Everybody has to get away from here."

The other men crowded around to listen.

"You have news from Simon Billings?" John

Robinson asked.

"I heard his boys talking," Eliza said, her voice filled with urgency. "I was picking up a load of grain. I came as fast as I could."

"Jennie!" John Robinson shouted immediately, running towards the house. "Bring the girls! Leave everything else! Get away from here!"

"We'll have to move all that powder from the barn!" Rudolf Werner said, as Eliza's words finally sunk in.

"There isn't time to move everything!" Eliza protested. "Get the horses out first."

"Right," Jeremy echoed. "There's a clearing back in the woods – we can take them down there."

"The muskets!" Abel Grimsby cried. "Don't let them capture our firearms!"

"Move the wagon," someone insisted. "That wagon's valuable!"

"We should stand and fight," Rudolf Werner proclaimed. "We men won't run!"

"We're not fools," Rodney Pringle argued. "Let's save ourselves now and fight later on."

As the hubbub swelled, Martin turned to Eliza and reached out to put a hand on her shoulder. "Thank you," he said simply. "Thank you for telling us."

Before Eliza could reply, Jeremy held up his hand for quiet. "Listen!" he said. "Someone's coming!"

They all froze, straining to hear. A distant rumble swelled to become the thunder of galloping hoofbeats. Everyone surged forward to look down the path.

For a breathtaking instant Eliza thought she had never seen anything so beautiful in all her life. The woods were aglow with bobbing lights, like the winking messages of giant fireflies. But these were not firefly lights; they were torches, carried by soldiers who marched up the path toward the farm. They were torches that would set fire to the house and barn. She couldn't see the soldiers, but she heard the steady pounding of their marching feet.

Well in advance of the troops came a lone rider on a big bay Conestoga. Even at a distance Eliza recognised his straight, bold posture and the way he held the reins. It was Ben.

Ben galloped toward the farm, with a hundred red-coated soldiers following behind him. He had led the British directly to his brother's hideout!

★ Chapter Twelve ★

The others rushed back to the barn, but Eliza and Jeremy stood frozen as Ben drew Hansel to a halt. Jeremy stared at him, too shocked to speak. But Eliza could not hold back.

"Stay away from us!" she screamed as Ben dismounted. "You're not my brother! You don't belong to our family any more!"

"Eliza—" Ben began.

She didn't let him finish. "How could you turn in your own brother? How could you—"

"Eliza!" Ben said again, "Stop it! You don't know what you're saying."

"I do too!" Eliza began to sob. "I know what you did!"

Ben's voice rose. "You've got the wrong idea, Eliza! I didn't tell the British anything. I came to warn Jeremy and his friends here."

Eliza opened her mouth to fling another barrage of anger in Ben's face. Then slowly, like raindrops on dry ground, his words began to seep in. "You... you *didn't* tell them?" she repeated. "But you—"

"I didn't," Ben said gently. "I heard talk on Delaware Ridge. I came here right away."

Jeremy seemed to waken from his trance. "Come on!" he said. "They're almost here!"

The lights swarmed closer. Eliza heard muffled voices and the tramp of boots.

The barn was a flurry of confusion. Martin and his father were rolling a barrel of powder out the door, blocking the way for Grimsby and Pringle as they tried to carry armloads of muskets. No one seemed to remember the horses.

"I'll get Maura," Eliza told her brothers. "Help me with the others."

"We don't have time to harness them up," Jeremy pointed out. "Anyway, we can't manage the wagon. We'll have to leave it here."

In seconds, Eliza was in Maura's stall, slipping a halter

over the top of her head. Maura shifted nervously, her tail swishing against the side of the stall. "Steady, girl," Eliza crooned. "We'll have you out of here in a minute."

Jeremy and Ben led out the rest of the team. Cricket, Annie and Zeke stamped and snorted, quivering on the edge of fear. There was too much noise and uncertainty at a time when they should have been enjoying peace and fresh hay. They knew that something was dreadfully wrong.

"Let's put them in formation," Eliza suggested. "It's what they're used to."

Ben shook his head doubtfully, but Jeremy understood at once. He moved Cricket into place behind Maura, and brought Zeke to stand at her right. Ben manoeuvred Annie into her position next to Cricket. Without their bells or harness, the four big Conestogas stood ready to haul a load of grain.

Eliza clicked her tongue and gave Maura's halter a gentle tug. Obediently Maura followed her. Just as Eliza had hoped, the other horses fell into step as though they were pulling a phantom wagon. The men cleared a path for them as they left the barn and headed for the woods. Among the trees the horses could no longer hold their tight formation. Yet they remained calm, and

Eliza and her brothers herded them down the hill to the clearing.

As soon as the team was safe, Eliza rushed back for Clipper. He waited with nostrils flaring and ears cocked, searching the air for hints of whatever lay ahead. She led him to join the others. Ben had brought Hansel to the clearing as well, and the six horses whickered and touched noses excitedly.

By now the men from the camp had taken refuge in the woods. Jennie Robinson was there, tense and tearful, clutching Evie and Abigail by their hands. The dog barked in the distance, still on guard at the empty house.

"Don't stand in a cluster!" John Robinson ordered. "Spread out! Scatter! Keep low!" There was no more talk about fighting, Eliza noted. Even John Robinson knew they were outnumbered.

Ben joined John Robinson, circling through the woods to be sure everyone was safe and accounted for. Jeremy and Eliza stayed in the clearing and tried to keep the horses calm. They could hear shouts from the farm now, excited voices rising and falling. The dots of torchlight melted together into one glowing ball of red flame, and Eliza knew that the farmhouse was burning. The breeze brought the smell of smoke, and the horses pranced nervously. "We've got to keep them quiet," Jeremy whispered. "If they make noise they'll give us away."

Eliza moved from one horse to another, stroking their flanks, murmuring close to their ears. Zeke and Cricket were jumpy and taut, ready to bolt at any moment. Clipper remained calm but alert, and Eliza hoped his presence would steady the others.

Suddenly a great tower of flame lit the sky, and there was a fierce, crackling roar. *The barn!* Eliza thought. *The powder!* Then, without further warning, the world seemed to heave and splinter, to explode in a burst of light and thunder. Men shouted, horses screamed in terror, but the roar of the blast drowned every other sound.

When Eliza opened her eyes she expected to see trees uprooted and the earth itself cracked and wounded. To her amazement the woods looked unchanged, and the ground was still solid beneath her feet. But the farm was a sea of flame. The figures of men dashed about in a sinister dance of triumph.

Zeke and Cricket were gone, crashing in panic through the woods. Annie and Hansel milled about in the clearing, and Jeremy held Maura by her halter, trying to keep her under control. Clipper's flanks heaved as though he'd just completed a twelve-mile haul, but he stood still in spite of the upheaval all around him.

There was another explosion, smaller this time, but it was too much for Annie and Hansel. Hansel gave a wild, high shriek of fright and bolted into the woods with Annie at his heels.

From the farm erupted a fresh burst of shouting. "They're out there!" came a clear voice. "Fire, boys!"

Shots rang out, a series of sharp reports above the roar of the burning buildings. A musketball thudded into a tree trunk a few yards from Eliza's head. She threw herself to the ground, remembering John Robinson's warning to keep low. More shots tore the air, and she flung her arms protectively over her head. *How can this be happening?* she thought in terror. This could be the end of everything she had ever known in her fourteen years on earth.

For a long time she lay motionless, and it took a moment to realise that there was no more musket fire. The crackling roar still came to her on the wind, and she heard a distant crash as something collapsed and fell. Those sounds of destruction seemed strangely removed. Close around her lay a thick blanket of silence.

"Get up!" Jeremy cried, breaking Eliza out of her daze. "We've got to catch the horses!"

Eliza staggered to her feet. "Where are the others?" she asked. "Is everyone all right?"

"Probably," Jeremy assured her, as they hurried into the woods. "I don't think the soldiers saw any of us. They were just firing at random."

It was easy to track the runaway horses. They had left a trail of trampled bushes and broken branches as they hurtled through the woods. Eliza and Jeremy found them one by one, and managed to herd them back to the clearing. Frightened as they were, the horses seemed to feel safer with trusted humans close by. They bunched tightly in the clearing, still skittish yet under control.

A twig snapped in the woods, and Eliza jumped. She half-expected a red-coated soldier to emerge, sighting along his musket barrel. Instead it was Abel Grimsby, looking pale and shaken. He opened his mouth to tell them something, but for a moment the words seemed locked in his throat. "Your brother's been hit," he croaked at last. "And Martin – Martin Robinson…"

"What happened?" Jeremy prompted. "Where's Martin now?"

Grimsby turned his face to the sky. "He's in

Heaven, I hope," he said. "The dirty Redcoats hit him square in the chest."

"Martin?" Jeremy repeated, aghast. "You mean he's dead?"

Grimsby nodded. "His father found him. He's lost almost everything tonight – his house, his barn, and his only son."

"What about Ben?" Eliza asked anxiously. "How bad is he hurt?"

"I don't know," Grimsby said. "He's back in there." He pointed off to the left.

Eliza and Jeremy hurried into the woods. Eliza imagined Ben crumpled and bloody, fighting for each breath as his life ebbed away, but, to her relief he wasn't so badly injured. They found him perched on a low tree limb, with someone's shirt wrapped around his left shoulder.

"It just grazed me," he told them. "Pringle says the bullet didn't touch the bone."

"We have to get away from here," Jeremy said, anxiously. "When they're tired of watching the fires, they'll come looking for us."

"Yes," Eliza said. "And then they won't be shooting at random."

"Whoever gave us away," Grimsby said bitterly, "he must be proud of himself tonight."

"It was old Mr Beekman," Ben explained. "I saw him, strutting like a peacock at the front of the column."

Of course! Eliza remembered the sly look on Peter Beekman's face when he told her, *I hear things when people don't think I'm listening.* She remembered his satisfaction when he told her that the rebels would all hang for treason. Of course Peter Beekman had betrayed them. Why had she ever suspected her own brother Ben? Ben had come to help – and been hit by a ball from a British musket!

"We've lost most of our muskets and powder," Jeremy said, "but we still have the horses. They can get us out of here."

Quickly and quietly, they searched the woods around the clearing, fanning out until everyone had been found. It was Eliza who came upon Jennie Robinson, cradling Martin's broken, blood-drenched body and crying silently. John stood beside her, stone-faced with anger and grief, while Evie and Abigail clung together, sobbing. Eliza averted her face hastily. She'd seen death often before – funerals were all too common around Judsonville, with fevers and agues taking their toll summer and winter. But she'd never before seen someone who had been killed by a bullet.

How can Martin Robinson be dead? Eliza asked herself in shock. Only this morning he had been so fierce and defiant! How was it possible that he could be gone so suddenly? She knew Martin had never liked her, and she had always been wary of him. Still, when she brought her warning tonight he had paused to thank her. Maybe they would have grown to trust each other over time. If he had lived, would they ever have become friends?

Eliza wished she could have left the Robinsons in peace – but there would be no peace, with the Redcoats on the prowl.

"Come back to the clearing," she said gently. "We have to go now. We'll put Martin on one of the horses and take him with us."

John Robinson touched his wife's shoulder. Together they lifted Martin's body and followed Eliza back to the horses, the little girls trailing behind them.

"Where's a place where all can be safe?" Rudolf Werner asked when they had gathered in the clearing. He glanced toward John Robinson, but their leader was too shattered to make any decision.

"I think," Ben said cautiously, "we should go to our place."

Eliza stared at him in amazement. Had his wound addled his brain? Did he really think Papa would shelter a pack of rebels?

"It is good," Mr Werner said, nodding. "Your papa has been very loyal to the king. No one will suspect him."

Eliza looked at Jeremy. Their eyes met. *Can we?* Eliza asked with her glance. And Jeremy's look answered, *We'll give it a try.*

⋆ Chapter Thirteen ⋆

At first they tried to have Hansel carry Martin's body, but the big bay gelding reared back with a low, rumbling neigh that was almost a growl. The smell of blood filled him with terror.

"You ride him," Eliza suggested to Ben. "Let Clipper carry Martin."

Clipper trembled for a moment when Rudolf Werner and John Robinson approached him, holding Martin's body between them. He stood patiently while they draped the dead boy over the saddle, and Eliza knew he would be all right. Shaken though she was by the events of the evening, she was proud that Clipper could be the horse for the task. She led him by the halter as they started out. John Robinson walked alongside, lost in grief.

There was no question of taking the regular path. The Redcoats would still be milling around the burning farm buildings and watching the path to the Judsonville road. The rebels would have to cut through the woods and meet up with the road further down. "We can take the deer trail," Jeremy said, and Eliza knew exactly what he meant. It was narrow and winding, but it allowed the horses to travel among the trees with relative ease. Some people rode and some walked. When they spoke they whispered. No one had much to say.

The underbrush and fallen leaves muffled the tramp of the horses' hooves. The trail was not a shortcut. It might add an hour to their journey, but safety was more important than speed. No Redcoat would know how to slip through these woods. *The British are foreigners*, Eliza thought. They didn't understand the land that was Pennsylvania.

She was in no hurry to reach home, Eliza admitted to herself as they forded a narrow stream. What would Papa say when a troop of rebels arrived at the door in the middle of the night? What would he do when he saw that they carried a dead boy, and that his own son was wounded?

Papa had always followed the rules. She had never heard him question the Crown's authority. Now they would be asking him to keep secrets, to hide rebels, and to accept that his own children – Ben included – were entangled with the rebel cause. Eliza wanted to believe the Carter home would be a haven for the rebels – especially for the Robinsons, who had lost so much. Yet she couldn't help but worry that Papa might decide that the right thing to do would be to turn the rebels in.

The moon shone high and bright when they emerged from the woods at last and struck out along the road. Holding the reins with his good hand, Ben let Hansel break into a trot. The other horses followed – all except Clipper. Slowly and solemnly he brought up the rear of the ragged little procession. It was as though he understood that he must carry his burden with dignity and care.

To Eliza's surprise, two Carter Distribution Company wagons stood in the wagon yard. She had expected to see only Hansel's wagon, since she had left Clipper's with the Werners. Before she could sort out what must have happened, Papa and Mama emerged from the house. Eliza saw Papa's gaze take everything in – the horses, the men and boys of the rebel band, the body sprawled across Clipper's saddle. His gaze fell on Eliza for a moment, and then passed her by. It came to rest on Jeremy.

"Jeremy!" Papa cried. "You're home! At last!"

Mama threw her arms around him. "Do you have any idea?" she kept saying. "Any idea at all?" She didn't have to explain what she meant; it was clear in her joyful relief.

The time had come, however, for other explanations. "Who's been hurt?" Papa asked Eliza. "What happened?"

"The Redcoats fired into the woods," she told him. "They hit Ben in the shoulder, but he's all right. Martin Robinson – he was killed."

"Killed?" Papa repeated as he looked more closely at the body on Clipper's back. "Oh my God!"

"Papa," Jeremy said, "all of us need a place to stay tonight. A safe place. The Redcoats will be looking for us."

Papa didn't take in Jeremy's words. He was still looking at Martin, his legs dangling lifelessly down Clipper's flank. "They fired into the woods?" he said again. "There were children there! They could have hit anyone!"

Jeremy nodded. "I thought they'd come looking for us after they fired," he said. "I don't know what stopped them."

"They're cowards; that's what it is," Abel Grimsby broke in. "They're afraid of the deep woods."

Papa walked over to the Robinsons. They were huddled together by the wagons, looking tired and scared and unimaginably sad. Papa held out his hand to John Robinson. "I'm so sorry," he said. "Is there anything we can do to help?"

Mama turned her attention to Ben, whose face was drawn with pain. "Does it hurt a lot?" she asked.

"Not much," Ben assured her, but he winced whenever he moved.

Mama led him aside and made him unwrap his shoulder for her inspection. "We'll need to clean it out some more," she said, frowning. "It could have been so much worse though! Thank goodness you're safe!"

"Pour a little whiskey on it," Rudolf Werner advised. "It will keep out the poison."

Ben's face twisted at the thought, but he didn't argue. "And I'll make you some comfrey tea," Mama said, fighting to sound cheerful. "You're going to be fine."

Papa was conferring with the men. Eliza heard Mr Werner say something about not wanting to put him in danger, but Papa merely shrugged.

"It will only be for a night or two," Abel Grimsby said. "We have to keep moving. There are others gathering in other towns – we'll be joining them."

Papa nodded. "Don't tell me any more," he said. "If they question me, the less I know, the better."

After a while Papa came back to Mama and said quietly, "We're going to bury the boy up in the pasture. Bring us a good linen sheet to wrap him in, all right?"

"Of course," Mama said, "but shouldn't he have a proper funeral, with a preacher?"

"I wish he could," Papa sighed. "But we have to keep this to ourselves."

Jeremy and Eliza led the horses into the barn and settled them in their stalls. Eliza was thrilled to find Zeus, April and Tillie there to greet her. When she emerged, she saw that Harriet and Mrs Werner had joined the group in the yard. Mary stood close beside them, staring with round, frightened eyes.

Harriet threw her arms around Eliza the moment she saw her. For a few moments they simply held each other, drawing comfort from their long years of friendship. "Your papa invited us to stay here," Harriet explained. "He came looking for you when it got dark. Mama was so worried, she ended up telling him where you'd gone."

"What did Papa say?" Eliza asked.

Harriet gave a tired grin. "He thought about it for a while, and then he said, 'Well, she does what needs to be done. She's got courage!'" Weary and troubled though she was, Eliza felt a glow of happiness.

The men finished digging a grave at the far end of the pasture. Ben and Jeremy joined Papa and Mr Werner, Grimsby and John Robinson as pallbearers. On a plank they carried Martin's body, wrapped in a sheet from Mama's linen chest, while everyone else filed behind. Papa read some verses from the Bible and they laid Martin Robinson in the ground.

Jeremy walked beside Eliza on the way back to the house. "He was a good friend," he said. "I can't tell you how much I'm going to miss him."

"For tonight," Papa announced, "the men can sleep in the loft over the grain warehouse."

"Thank you, Papa," Jeremy said fervently. "Thank you!"

"It's not a matter of choice," Papa said. "We all have

to help each other now."

"You mean," Jeremy asked cautiously, "you'll help us resist the British?"

"When the king's men will burn farms and fire into the woods to kill us…" Papa paused, struggling to put his thoughts into words. "When they treat us like this," he concluded, "they force us to fight back."

Mama put her arms around him. "It's not easy to change your mind," she said. "I'm proud of you."

Mama spent a while with Jennie Robinson, helping her settle Evie and Abigail in with Mary. On any other night the three girls would have been giggling and chattering with delight. Now they were subdued and pale.

At last, all of their unexpected guests were settled in for what remained of the night, and the Carters were alone together. They sat in the drawing room and talked in the flickering candlelight.

"We've crossed a line tonight," Papa said, looking each one of them in the eye. "Once Penn realises that I've taken the rebels' side, he'll do everything he can to ruin our business."

"Do you think that we should start over somewhere else?" Mama asked gently. "In the Susquehanna country, maybe?"

"We could," Papa said. "There are plenty of farmers out there now with grain to haul." He was quiet for a few moments, looking down at his hands. When he spoke again, his voice was firm. "But it wouldn't be right to turn and run now. We're colonists; we need to stay and support the cause."

"We can keep the business going without any help from Governor Penn," Ben declared. "More and more farmers are ready to break ties with the British."

"Especially after tonight," Eliza added. "By tomorrow, everyone in the valley will be whispering about what happened."

"We need to spread the word beyond the valley," Papa said. "The Continental Congress should hear about what happened. I'm tempted to go to Philadelphia when they meet, to tell the story myself."

"What about Maura?" Jeremy asked suddenly. "The governor will be coming to get her team and wagon."

Papa looked resolute. "It looks like I can't spare any of my teams after all," Papa said with an ironic laugh. "We had a gentleman's agreement. I don't think it holds now, under the circumstances."

"Maura won't ever have to haul for the Redcoats!"

Jeremy said with relief. "I couldn't stand the thought of it!"

"We all need to get some sleep," Mama said gently. "We have a lot to do in the morning."

Eliza and Jeremy exchanged a glance. Eliza read that Jeremy was as wide awake as she was. "I feel as if my mind is on fire," she told him.

"I know," Jeremy whispered back. "I feel the same way." *Of course you do*, Eliza thought. *And not just because we're twins.*

Quietly they slipped out of the house as the others made ready for bed. It couldn't hurt to check on the horses one more time.

Eliza found Clipper dozing in his stall, head lowered and legs wide apart. As soon as he heard her voice he came alert and stretched his head toward her over the door. She traced his white blaze lightly with her fingertips. "Oh, Clipper," she murmured, "what a wonderful horse you are!"

"He got you to the Robinson place just in time," Jeremy said beside her. "If you hadn't warned us, they'd have caught us all at the forge."

"We took the shortcut from the Werners," Eliza said. "I wish you could have seen him sliding down the ravine!"

"He's a horse you can rely on," Jeremy said. "The best of the best."

"I was afraid sometimes," Eliza admitted. "After you left I felt as though our family was tearing apart."

"We're together now," Jeremy said as he turned to head back into the house. "The way we're supposed to be."

Eliza gave Clipper a parting hug. "It's almost tomorrow already," she told him. "Rest up. We have a lot of hard hauling ahead of us."

To whet your appetite for another thrilling adventure in the Saddle the Wind *series, read on for the opening chapter of* Riding the Pony Express.

★ SADDLE THE WIND ★

RIDING THE PONY EXPRESS

DEBORAH KENT

WYOMING, 1861
AND THE PONY EXPRESS TRAIL IS FULL OF PERIL...

When her father dies suddenly, fifteen-year-old Lexie
McDonald is left an orphan. Her brother, Callum, is on
the run, accused of a crime he didn't commit, and now
Lexie is to be sent to live with an aunt in New York.
Rather than be separated from her beloved horse,
Cougar, Lexie makes the bravest decision of her life.
Secretly, and disguised as a boy, she sets out with
Cougar along the dangerous Pony Express trail, to find
Callum and clear his name.

⋆ Chapter One ⋆

"I will lift up mine eyes unto the hills, from whence cometh my help," intoned Reverend Harkness. "My help cometh from the Lord, who made the heaven and the earth…"

Lexie McDonald gazed at the ring of peaks looming above her. *Reverend Harkness can talk all he wants,* she thought, *but there is no help from the hills today.* The reverend's words rattled around her, as dry and lifeless as kindling.

A gust of wind whipped through the crowd of mourners. Mrs Harkness clapped one hand onto her bonnet and tried to hold it in place, all the time looking solemn and proper, as if nothing was amiss. For an instant,

Lexie thought of turning to Papa with raised eyebrows, sharing a bemused moment. Not even the Wyoming wind could ruffle the dignity of Mrs Harkness.

In the next instant the truth crashed in on her again, as it had a thousand times over the past two days. Papa wasn't standing beside her. She would never see him again. Reverend Harkness was performing the funeral service beside Papa's newly-dug grave.

Even now she couldn't quite believe that Papa lay sleeping in that narrow pine box that Will Jenkins had hammered together yesterday morning. All of these people – the whole town of Willow Springs, in fact – had gathered for his funeral, yet to Lexie nothing felt real. At any moment she expected Papa to step up beside her with a mischievous grin and beckon her to follow him. She'd slip away, right from under the watchful eyes of Mrs Harkness, and laugh with him about how he'd fooled everyone into thinking he was dead and gone. "They can't get rid of me that easy!" he'd say. "Not a tough old guy like me!"

"Now let us repeat the Lord's Prayer," Reverend Harkness said. Lexie folded her hands and added her voice to the murmur around her. The familiar words caught in her throat, and she fell silent by the time they came to "forgive us our trespasses". *I'm not going to cry,* she told herself fiercely. *Not now, in front of all these people! Papa would want me to be strong!*

The prayer came to an end. Reverend Harkness uttered some phrases about "ashes to ashes, dust to dust", and the first handfuls of earth thudded onto the lid of the coffin. Mrs Harkness turned to Lexie. "Come on, dear," she said in a low voice. "We'll all go back to the parsonage for a little something to eat."

Food was the last thing on Lexie's mind. Nothing could comfort her but a long ride on her buckskin gelding, Cougar. "I'm really not hungry, thank you," she said. "I'd like to be by myself for a while."

Mrs Harkness clicked her tongue and frowned. "All these people came to pay their respects to your father," she said. "It's your duty to show some appreciation."

Already, Lexie was learning that she couldn't argue when Mrs Harkness had made up her mind. "Yes, I know," she said. "I'm grateful that everyone came. I really am."

It was wonderful to see that so many people cared about

her father, Lexie reflected as she followed Mrs Harkness along Main Street. Over and over, people had told her how much they would miss him, and they meant what they said. The Scotsman Rob McDonald had been a mainstay in the community. For ten years he'd run the general store, selling nails, twine, feed, sugar, and salt to the settlers for twenty miles around. During the past year he'd been a stationmaster for the Russell, Majors, and Waddell company that ran the Pony Express – the company was determined to provide the most reliable mail service available, and Papa had respected their strict ethical values. The Pony Express was about good men providing the best service possible – through rain, snow, sleet, and hail – and Papa had admired their determination.

As the Willow Springs stationmaster, stabling horses and readying them for each relay rider who galloped in, Papa was known for almost fifty miles up the trail east and west for his good humour, his fairness, and his honesty. It became one of Papa's passions that, one day, the Pony Express would become the official mail carrier for the United States, and so he dutifully played his part in getting the mail delivered on time. No wonder so many people had put aside their work and come to say their last goodbyes.

"I suppose you'll want to get the rest of your things from the station," Mrs Harkness said as they walked along. "Some little keepsakes for your new room."

"I'll ride over there later," Lexie said. "But I won't be staying long at the parsonage."

Mrs Harkness eyed her doubtfully. "It could be weeks till we hear from your aunt back east. And if the snow comes early and the passes are closed, you might be with us till next spring."

"It's very kind of you to have me," Lexie said. The reverend and his wife meant well, but Lexie couldn't imagine staying with them all winter long! Just another three days under their roof would drive her crazy – and moving to New York City, a place she'd never been, to live with an aunt she'd never met would be much worse. She couldn't let them send her east; somehow she had to think of a way out!

At the little clapboard house that Willow Springs called the parsonage people were already gathering. A few neighbour women were in the kitchen, loading platters with bread and meat and pies. They greeted Lexie sympathetically and urged her to eat, but she thanked them and shook her head. "Go and sit in the parlour," Mrs Harkness told her. "People will want to offer their condolences."

Slowly, her feet as heavy as stone, Lexie left the kitchen. She didn't know what to say to all those sorry, sombre people. She wasn't sure she could answer them without bursting into tears. She paused outside the kitchen door, bracing herself for the ordeal ahead, when behind her she heard one of the women say, "He was such a fine man! So hardworking and steady!"

Lexie lingered to listen. She treasured every word in praise of her father. In some small way those kind remembrances brought him back to her. "He took sick so suddenly!" Lexie recognised the nervous, fluttery voice of May Jenkins, the carpenter's wife. "Tuesday I heard he was down with a pain in his belly, and Wednesday he was gone."

"My husband says it was the trouble over Callum that killed him," said Mrs Harkness. "That boy broke his father's heart. But the traits were there; they were bound to come out."

Lexie tensed as she listened.

"Alexandra, she's different," May Jenkins said. "She's as pretty as any white girl. You'd hardly guess—"

"It shows a bit in her face," Mrs Harkness said. "And the straight black hair, of course. But mostly she takes after her father, thank heavens!"

"That boy," May Jenkins said with a sigh. "The first time I saw him I took him for a full-blooded Indian!"

"They couldn't keep him in school, you know," another voice chimed in. "Any chance he got he was out the door, riding off to who knows where on some half-wild bronco."

"I wasn't surprised when I heard about the business with the mail pouch," May Jenkins said. "What else can you expect?"

"He'll hang if they ever catch him," Mrs Harkness said with a hint of satisfaction. "But don't tar Alexandra with the same brush. Once she settles down, she'll be a proper young lady."

Lexie's stomach lurched. She had heard more than enough. She couldn't bear to spend another moment at the parsonage now. Without a word to anyone, she slipped through the back door and dashed to the field behind the house.

The wind had risen, and the late summer air was crisp and cool. Trying to steady herself, Lexie breathed in the familiar smells of hay and wildflowers. She hadn't cried at the funeral, but now, at last, her eyes burned with tears. How dare they speak like that about Callum on the same day as Papa's funeral! Nothing could hurt Papa more than cruel words about his son. And how dare they talk about Indian blood as though it was a curse. "As pretty as any white girl!" she repeated, almost choking on the words. "I don't want to be like any white girl!" she cried. "Not if it means growing up to be like them."

Not far from the barn, Mrs Harkness's chestnut mare, Hattie, grazed quietly. Cougar was farther off, near a cluster of piñon pines. When Cougar was a colt, Lexie had trained him to come when she gave the lonesome whistle of the mountain quail. It had been a chance to teach him loyalty and obedience, a way to strengthen the bond between them. Now she tilted back her head and gave the quail's low, clear whistle. Cougar lifted his head and trotted toward her with light, eager steps.

✫

Lexie leaned against Cougar's shoulder. He stood still and solid, unshakable in the midst of her turmoil. She slid her arms around his neck and felt his warm, smooth hide against her tear-stained cheek. "Oh, Cougar," she moaned. "I'm an orphan now! What am I going to do?" Cougar twisted his head around to nuzzle her hair. In the only way he could he seemed to be assuring her that everything would be all right.

Lexie had lost all of the people she had ever loved. A sudden, terrible illness had snatched away her father. Her brother, Callum, had fled town six months ago, accused of stealing a valuable package from the Pony Express mail. Her mother, the woman who gave the McDonald children their Arapaho blood, had died when Lexie was only five. Only Cougar was left, and if the reverend and his wife sent her to Aunt Grace McDonald, Cougar would have to stay behind in Wyoming Territory. She would lose him, too.

By now, Mrs Harkness had probably noticed that she wasn't sitting in the parlour. They were sure to send someone searching for her. She would have to move fast if she was going to get her ride.

*

Hurrying to the barn, Lexie lifted Cougar's saddle from the rack. It was a boy's saddle, not a lady's sidesaddle like the one that Mrs Harkness used for sedate little rides on Hattie. Lexie was still wearing the long, black skirt that Mrs Harkness had lent her for the funeral. It was completely unsuitable for riding astride. She had made herself a divided skirt that allowed her to ride with almost as much ease and freedom as a boy, but it was still back at the station. It was one of the things that she wanted to collect and bring back to the parsonage.

Lexie hadn't been able to take Cougar out for a run since the day Papa got sick. Now he was "wound tight as a spring," as Papa would say. As Lexie saddled him up, he neighed playfully to Hattie. *It's as if he's telling her he wished she could come along too*, Lexie thought. Cougar had always been friendly with other horses, ready to play whenever he had the chance. Maybe it was because he'd missed out on being with other colts when he was growing up.

Lexie put a foot in the stirrup and flung her other leg across Cougar's back. She gathered the black skirt out of the way as well as she could and picked up the reins. She didn't have to nudge him ahead with her heels. As soon as she was in the saddle, Cougar set off for the hills at a brisk trot.

Three years ago, when she was twelve, Lexie had found Cougar in a sagebrush hollow, trembling beside the bloodied body of his mother. Lexie had ridden out that day on Callum's bay gelding, Ranger, to watch the herd of wild mustangs that had been grazing there for weeks. But the herd was gone, all but the spindly-legged buckskin colt and the fallen mare. The colt hadn't wanted to leave his mother, but Lexie coaxed him to follow her back to town, holding out her fingers for him to suck on. He seemed to take comfort from her presence, and from that day on he had been her horse in such a special way. They had each lost their mother when they were very young, and Lexie felt that they shared an invisible bond of understanding.

"Sounds like it was a mountain lion – a cougar – that killed the mare," Papa had said when he saw the colt and heard Lexie's story. "No wonder the rest of the herd ran off."

Lexie had never seen a live cougar, but once a rancher rode into town to collect a bounty on one he'd shot.

Draped limply across the rancher's saddle, it was both sinister and beautiful. Its body was lithe and golden, graceful even in death. Its dead claws raked the empty air, and its razor-sharp teeth snarled at the curious crowd.

She was aghast when Callum suggested that she give the name "Cougar" to the colt. "Never!" Lexie exclaimed. "Why should he live with the reminder of what happened? He should have a bright, happy name to help him forget."

Papa shook his head thoughtfully. "Callum has a point," he told her. "This colt got off to a rough start in life. Some horses don't recover from a thing like that. It leaves them skittish, and you can never count on them. Your mother's people say there's power in a name. If you call the colt Cougar, maybe he'll find the strength to get over his fear."

Perhaps the name had worked magic. Cougar was high-spirited, even willful at times, but he wasn't skittish. Once when a jackrabbit leaped up right under his hooves, he hadn't even flinched. He'd grown up to be a horse that she could count on, and he'd become her best friend. Now he was all she had left...